I0537830

AND OTHER INSANE TALES

(An anthology of the strange, bizarre, and just plain weird)

JEN WYLIE
SEAN HAYDEN

Untold
Press

FLASHY FICTION AND OTHER INSANE TALES
VOLUME 1
An Untold Press Anthology
First Printing, May 2012

Published by Untold Press LLC
114 NE Estia Lane
Port St Lucie, FL 34983
www.untoldpress.com

ISBN: 978-0-61563-143-1

PRODUCED IN THE UNITED STATES OF AMERICA

10 9 8 7 6 5 4 3 2 1

Dedication

From Jen Wylie

I'd like to dedicate what I've written to my sister and her wonderful new husband. May your lives be flashy, but never too insane!

From Sean Hayden

I'd like to dedicate these words to the three best friends anyone could have had growing up. Chad, Erin, and Dennis, you stood by me through thick and thin, forgave me at my worst, and got me into more trouble than I can remember. For that, I will *always* thank you!

Special Thanks

Both authors would like to give sincere thanks to a wonderfully amazing lady, Donna. She not only proofread each story in this series and gave us her opinions, but provided the dining room table for the authors to work on. Not to mention the pickled eggs.

Contents

Zombies at the Meat Market

by

Sean Hayden

Another Saturday night, and I friggin' get stuck workin'. I did have grand plans to spend the night at home watching movies, but no. I get called into work.

Sometimes I hated being a butcher, and I've always hated the lazy ass people I work with. They get scheduled to work Saturdays, and then they call in sick. Whiney maggots.

Saturdays at the grocery store really, truly suck ass in Florida. The only people shopping after dark are the lonely old people from the retirement communities who think supermarkets are the equivalent of a singles club. Now I get to rush into work and get pawed by the blue hairs. Ever hand somebody a T-bone and they caress your hand when you do it? It isn't pleasant.

To top everything off, because I was in such a rush, I forgot my damn contacts. Now all I could do was pray I didn't slice off a finger in the bone saw.

I grumble to myself the entire way into work. At least I don't live far away which is both a blessing and a curse. Why do managers feel less guilty calling in the people who live closer? Like you're less of an asshole because I have to drive five minutes less than anybody else? Seems pretty fair to me. Maybe I'll move to Toledo. That should put me on the last to call list, right? Probably not. Seems like I'm the only one stupid enough to answer their phone on a Saturday night.

The only comforting thing about going to work is the frigid air that blasts you in the face when the automatic doors open with a happy little swoosh. Florida heat is more oppressive than a dictator with hemorrhoids. People actually run from their cars to get inside the stores. It would be pretty funny to watch if you didn't have to stand outside to see it. What's really funny is grocery stores are a little colder than every other sort of retail location, probably due to the amount of elderly consumers gracing our halls with their little electric carts. They must think lowering the temperature will lengthen the lifespan of the average retired consumer. More likely it's to keep the smell down.

Mark Johnson, the store manager, waved at me when I walked by. I gave him the finger and finished tying the strings on my white apron. I looked down at the multitude of pinkish stains and found myself wondering what idiot came up with white as the universal butcher uniform. One day I would find out his name and add it to my "fucktards who need a good bitch slappin'" blog.

I pushed open the flappy door that led to my own personal domain and nodded at Nick, the other unlucky bastard who seemed to get the shit end of the stick almost as much as me.

"That little snot nosed prick Ted call in sick?"

"Of course he did. He still lives with his mom and dad so he doesn't give a damn if he gets fired. I swear to God, Nick, one more time and I'm outta here."

"Yeah sure, I think you've said that the last five times, big guy. Have fun tonight. Oh, and be careful. I think I saw Edna on Aisle 5. She *likes* you!"

"Great," I said and dropped my forehead to the cold glass covering the chops and steaks. I waved a half-hearted goodbye to Nick as I heard him laughing on his way out of the meat department.

Edna was the bane of the meat department's better looking staff. She was about ninety-five and had more hair on her face than most truckers I've met, or even seen on television. She even had one of those moles that had hair that just never seemed to stop growing straight out of it. It must be a bitch to eat soup with one of those. The really *icky* thing about Edna is every time she came up to the meat counter she'd ask to smell things before she bought them. Not too unusual, but she held on to your hands while she brought her face up across the counter and made noises like a just released cocaine addict scoring an eight-ball.

"Attention Meat Department, truck delivery on the loading dock." Mark Johnson's voice rang ominously over the intercom.

Perfect. I briefly wondered if Nick would take pity on me and give me a hand unloading the truck. Very briefly. Nick was okay, but I knew what I would do if the situation were reversed. I'd leave him in a heartbeat.

I trudged my way into the back and sure enough, Toothless Eddy was standing at the back door of his truck which he had expertly backed up to the loading dock.

"Hiya, kid. Workin' again, huh?" Eddie smiled his toothless grin that never ceased to amuse me. It was like his nose became a black hole that swallowed the rest of his features. Toothless Eddie really did have teeth. The only problem is they sat on the dashboard of his Semi. I know because I saw them once.

"Yeah, lucky me," I said with a sigh and started pulling the carts into the enormous walk in freezer. Technically I should break everything down and package it into little shrink wrapped Styrofoam containers. Technically I should be sitting at home watching movies, too. "Frozen till morning," that's my motto.

I signed off on Eddy's delivery and coughed at the puff of diesel smoke his rig left as he pulled away. Poor bastard still had three deliveries to make before he got to go home, and he'd been working since this morning. Suddenly my job didn't seem too bad, Edna and all.

From the back of the prep area I could see a crowd of people standing at the meat counter. I sighed and grabbed a towel to wipe my hands with. They weren't dirty, but I learned if you walked out from the back wiping your hands, people nodded at you like the understood you were busy. Cheap trick, but it worked. I tossed the towel on the counter and grabbed the little electronic ticker that kept track of which customer I was serving. I looked at the back wall to see what number I was on but had to squint to see the numbers. It was 33, 38, 83, or 88. Without my contacts I couldn't tell, but due to the average age of my regular clientele, I would bet even money they couldn't either.

"Now serving, eighty-three!" I looked out at the crowd in front of me. I couldn't make out any details of their faces without my contacts, but they looked rough. They even seemed, if at all possible, even older than my usual Saturday night crowd. Maybe the local nursing home carted up some of the residents for a "shopping" night instead of "movie and pudding" night.

Almost comically they all looked down at their hands before looking up and turning to their neighbor to see which lucky bastard had number "83". I saw a little hand in the back raise up and a, "Ugh," followed the hand. Ding, ding, ding we have a winner. The crowd parted and Edna walked through the sea of old people crowding the counter.

"Waaa uungh glaah," Edna called a little more articulately than usual over the counter. I've been working at the butcher shop in the grocery store for almost 8 years. Every time Edna came in she always asked for pork chops or chicken breasts. "Waa uungh glaah," sounded a little closer to pork chops than chicken breasts so I reached down and grabbed her usual two from the front of the display case. Holding them out to her over the counter I waited for the sniffing to begin and my stomach to start rolling. I tried very hard to think of kittens playing in a meadow.

I turned my head as I felt Edna's hands close around my wrists. I sighed when that happened. Edna's grip on your hands wasn't something that you could wash away easily. One of the kittens in my head was chasing dandelion puffs when Edna pulled me against the counter with the force of a tow truck dragging a Vespa scooter. I heard the glass case crack as the pork chops were yanked from my grip.

"What the fuck, Edna?" I stared angrily over the counter. I didn't care if the manager Mark Johnson was standing right behind me. That hurt like a son of a bitch.

I rubbed my chest and looked over at Edna who was chowing down on the pork chops right in front of me. I felt my stomach churn as I squinted to get a better look. Edna's usual grey pallor had been replaced by a sickly green one, and I could see the pork as it passed from her mouth to her esophagus by way of the large hole that had been torn in her throat. I looked at the other escapees from the nursing home and sure enough, some were missing eyes, some limbs, and the only thing in common was that not one of the bastards was alive.

It would absolutely positively figure. Only I could have the day off, get called into work, and end up being eaten by a roving horde of geriatric zombies.

I backed away from the glass display case and stood with my back against the cold tile of the wall behind me. Some of them started to climb over. The rest just started shattering the glass with their limbs and plowing through the meat. They didn't want ground chuck. They wanted me. I only hoped one of them got to me before Edna did.

"Sonofabitch."

There were zombies at my meat market.

A while ago, I started a flash fiction challenge for myself. I wanted to be challenged. I figured the best way to do that would be to have a topic thrown at me and to give myself a time limit to complete it. I had a rare *flash of brilliance! I had a multitude of twitter friends to draw upon. Every few days I would call out for a topic. The first person to reply was the winner. I had to write a short story by the end of the day and post it for them to read. The consequence for failure? I had to post a picture of myself on twitter in a dress. Needless to say I never lost!*

Zombies at the Meat Market was the first of the competition. The whole project even had a name. S.H.I.T.S, Sean Hayden's Inspired by Twitter Stories! I had a lot *of fun writing these. I hope you enjoy them!*

The Sweetest Vampire: A Sappy Story

by

Jen Wylie

Discussion Boards post 10385

Let's play a game. Can you figure out what I am? I hope so. I certainly don't know. I want to know, so very badly, I'm willing to risk myself in writing this.

As most people are aware, not knowing can be painful. Not in a physical sense, though consequences of ignorance can certainly result in such pain. I'm speaking about psychological pain, emotional pain, that pain of not knowing who you are, or even what you are.

Let's get to it, shall we? I want answers probably as much as you are dying to discover what I'm talking about.

I have been this way for a very long time. So long my memories of the past, of my making, have grown a bit foggy. Even so, that story isn't short, and those details do not pertain to the question at hand. We'll leave them for another day. Right now I am hoping someone out there knows what I am. I have so many questions; even just a few answers would be a blessing.

Back to the facts. You need details. I do know some things about myself of course. As these things about me aren't secrets I'll even tell them to you. Of course the amusing part of this is the multi-sided question I have posed to you. One answer I do know and the hints to it are part of what I will share with you. I'll let you guess. If you get it right I'll give you a cookie.

Shall we start at the beginning? For me, it's when the sun rises. I love the sun, need the sun, and without it I grow weary, weak. Darkness itself, shadows, don't actually bother me too much, as in they won't kill me. However I am at my full power standing under the glorious light of the risen sun.

Sunsets make me cry. More so in the past than recent times, though they still do. It's not just their beauty; it's the temporary draining of power. I hate feeling powerless. In this new modern age however, I do have some relief. I danced with joy when those specialty lights were invented. You know the ones that mimic sunlight, giving off all the appropriate rays and everything. My house if full of them, you should see my electric bill.

I see you're scratching your head. Let me tell you more about myself. I don't age. I don't get sick. Heat and cold, any type of weather, does not bother me. I actually quite enjoy a run through the snow. Physically, I look human, except for my pointed teeth.

I gave it away didn't I? One of the many answers to what I am. Yes, I am a vampire in the general sense of the word. I hate categorizing myself, but if the shoe fits... Obviously I'm not a normal one. What exactly I am I would really love to know. If it makes you feel better, I've never met another like myself, or even heard of one with my strange characteristics. Needing the sun is not the only thing different about me.

I don't drink blood; human, animal or anything in between. I never have, and never will. The thought of blood appalls me. Actually ingesting it would probably do me harm.

Yes, I do need to eat. I consider myself a vegetarian. My nourishment comes from plants. I could live off of grass, though I find it nasty and un-filling. Some vegetables aren't too bad. It is certainly easy to find food, there is always some store open or I can just take a wander outside and try the native flora.

You're picturing me browsing the produce aisle aren't you? Perhaps coming home and throwing together a veggie smoothie in the blender. Better yet, sinking my teeth into a juicy melon, or maybe a tomato, and having the red juice run down my chin. As amusing as that would be, you're ahead of yourself. Yes, I can live off of such things, but they don't make me strong, powerful.

Where does the most nourishing food come from? Trees of course, more specifically the energy filled, wondrous sap which flows within them. I do indeed frequent the grocery store, but it is the aisle which carries the maple syrup I go to. I'm not talking about that fake crap, no I'm after the *real* maple syrup, preferably not the light stuff either. I want the good stuff, the strong stuff. The condensed sugary goodness.

Does any of this help at all? Do you know what I am? If you have any idea, do feel free to shoot me an email. I'd certainly love to know. If by some chance you are like me, please do the same. Knowing I'm not alone would ease my sugary heart.

You still have a chance for a cookie. (A sugar cookie of course, with sprinkles.) There is one other thing you can guess about me. I've given you some clues. Have you figured it out yet?

No? Very well, I'll tell you...

I am Canadian.

Eh.

What can I say, I am Canadian! This short story was a bit of poking fun at that. I tend to get teased by my online American friends about my use of 'eh', my love of bacon, hockey sticks (I actually don't play hockey!) and of course my love of maple syrup.

Every Time I Walk into a Room

by

Sean Hayden

The *glurb, glurb, glurb* of the five gallon water bottle as I filled my tiny styrofoam cup was almost deafening in the silence that permeated the room. The sad thing was I wasn't alone. At least seven people filled the tiny break room at the "My Cup Runneth Over" brassiere factory where I have been employed for the last eight months. I know what you're thinking. Why would a woman demean herself by working for a company so obviously degrading to women? Overflowing cups didn't exactly scream, "Classy." The answer is easy, they pay extremely well and they have slick marketers. Everybody knows about and wears the MCRO bras, but only the employees know what the acronym stands for. As I said, the marketing department is pretty slick.

After what seemed to be an eternity, my cup was finally full of water. Without turning around I brought it up to my lips to take a drink. I could feel, or at least I thought I could feel, everybody's eyes glued to my back and the feeling wasn't pleasant. Not even a little bit. My heart starting beating faster and I could feel a cold sweat threatening to make my white shirt see through. I've never been one for the center stage. Don't get me wrong, everybody tells me I'm an attractive woman, but I've always been just a little more than a tad bit shy.

I couldn't take it anymore. I'm a patient person, but fourteen eyeballs boring little holes into my backside were a little more than I could handle. I spun in a half pirouette and came face to face with no one. I was completely alone in my little corner of paranoia hell. I giggled a little with relief and chalked the whole thing up to my imagination. I downed the rest of my water and crushed the Styrofoam cup in my hand like I was a burly beer drinker who had just finished a cold can of "Milwaukee's Beast". Heading out the door, I tossed it into the little bin next to the water cooler. Yes, I even gave a little fist pump.

My trudge back to my tiny little cubicle killed my mood faster than my last cholesterol test. Every time I passed by people in the walkway, they would stop talking. Something was definitely going on, I just couldn't tell what. It had been like that since I came in first thing this morning. They wouldn't laugh, or smile, just suddenly stop conversing until I passed. My heart sank. *Maybe I was getting fired? I hadn't screwed an order up had I?* I can tell you one thing. That didn't make for pleasant thoughts as I walked back to my desk. I started to shake a little as I picked up my headset and dialed into the queue of waiting sales calls.

"Hello, and thank you for calling MCRO, how can I help you?" Maybe if I just concentrated on work and did a good job "they" wouldn't fire me. That always works in the movies, right? The hard working girl, determined to make it in the harsh reality of the modern world, never gets fired right?

"Um, yes, I would like to place an order." A male voice breathed heavily in my earpiece. Ewww, this day just kept getting better and better.

"Sure, sir, what can I get for you," I said calmly into my tiny little microphone and brought up a fresh order page on my decrepit, stained in several places so it looked vaguely like a cow, computer.

"Oh, yeah," he said almost like he was out of breath. "I have to have a number 707535-A. Please God, give me number 707535-A," he said in a rising crescendo. I was starting to get a little weirded out.

"Is there anything else I can get for you today, sir?"

"NO. I mean, no thank you. Wow, that was incredible. Just the 707535-A," he said and started to sound

19

a little more normal as his breathing returned to a regular rhythm. *Ick*.

I took all his payment information, logged it in, and hung up with a quick, "Thank you for your purchase." I was a little proud of myself for leaving off the, "Slimeball," I wanted to add to the sentence. I needed another drink. Something a little stronger than water. No, I don't mean coffee, I needed a friggin' cocktail.

"Thank you for calling MCRO, how can I help you?"

"Yes, I'd like to order a 70735-A. It's for my wife," a man said on the other line. Something was strange. I usually had about one man a month call in to order something. Two in a row was unheard of, and both for the same product? I shrugged and finished the order. At least this customer didn't appear to be in the middle of *anything else* while he ordered.

"Thank you for calling MCRO, how can I help you?"

"Hello, I'd like to place an order," whispered the sultry voice of a woman this time. At least things were getting back to normal.

"Sure, what can I get for you?" I sounded almost chipper this time.

"I simply must have three 707535-A's, please," she said. I resisted the urge to let my head fall to the desk. Quickly I completed the order and logged off the phone system. I needed another drink even if it was just water. Things were just too weird today.

I stood up, pulled my skirt down to straighten it out and turned around. No less than three sets of eyes were peering at me from over the cubicle walls surrounding me. As soon as I opened my mouth to yell they all popped back behind the safety of their walls. I debated looking over the closest one and asking what was going on, but you just didn't do that. Your cubicle kept you safe from zombies, natural predators, and they were also rumored to spare your life in case of thermonuclear bombardment. At least that's what I heard.

I had *deja vu* as I walked back to the break room. Everybody stopped talking as I passed them in the hall, and the four people who were in the break room stood and left without uttering a single word as I crossed the threshold. Tears started to well up in my eyes. *What did I do?* I didn't recall running over any puppies with my car, I haven't murdered anyone (unless it was when I was drunk at the Christmas party last week). I even went to church last Sunday! Come on!

Then it dawned on me. The Christmas party! I vaguely remember a tryst in the copy room with one of the account execs. He must have told everybody about it! Angrily I clenched my fists as I thought of ways to slowly dismember him, microwave the pieces, and serve them as a break-room buffet. I'd have to find an extremely dull butter-knife to do it with. Maybe a spork would be better.

My hand was half way to the stack of cups sitting on top of the grey counter next to the water cooler when *he* walked in. I stopped and turned to go confront the spiky-haired blond buffoon and give him a piece (or several) of my mind. My leg hit one of the break room chairs and I glanced down at the table.

There on the cover of our latest sales flier was me. The angle of the photo was almost straight up. You could see my face in the throes of ecstasy, my hands squeezing my bra covered breasts. You could tell I was mid-orgasm. I vaguely remember laying over the office color copier/scanner with the exec behind me.

I picked up the flier and looked closer. I couldn't believe the face I was making, and my shirt was completely off. "At least I was wearing a bra," I muttered, looking on the bright side. Its MCRO satin label showed proudly and clearly on my very own 707535-A.

"How would you like to move from sales to modeling?"

This was another of my Sean Hayden's Inspired by Twitter Stories. "Every time I walk into a room" didn't exactly help! I had to really put on my thinking cap for this one and I think it was the closest I came to putting on a dress for a photoshoot! Inspiration struck me at the last moment. Thank you, Victoria's Secret catalog! You saved me!

The Sweetest Vampire: Bittersweet Memories

by

Jen Wylie

I wake with the sun, a smile coming to my face as its faint rising light entered my room through the windows. I have a lot of windows, not unusual for someone who adores the sun as much as I do. It's just very unusual for a vampire, but then again, I'm not a normal vampire. I love the sun. Darkness, shadows drain me. I don't drink blood either. I gain sustenance from plants, from the juices within them. My favorite is maple syrup, strong, thick and sweet, it gives me energy like nothing else does. I am also Canadian, if that matters or not. Sometimes it does, eh.

Stretching, I slip out of bed and draw on a light robe. Autumn has finally arrived and though the chill doesn't bother me, it is the human thing to do. I like to stay in practice, being discovered for what I am has never been a good thing.

My bare feet don't make a sound as I wander into the kitchen. It is a room I don't use often, so it is always neat and clean. I pull a bottle of syrup from the fridge and generously fill a mug and pop it into the microwave. While the machine whirs away I stare out the window, watching the sun as it fully slips above the horizon. The windows need cleaning again. I'll have to remember to call someone about that.

Beep, beep, beep. I hold back a yawn as I retrieve my warmed breakfast. The sweet syrup coats my mouth with the first sip and I find half the mug gone within moments. Energy courses within me, making me smile again. Yes, I smile a lot. I have reason to. I know I have a good life, an easy one.

I move to the living room and flip on the computer, checking my cell phone for messages while it boots up. There are none, which is not surprising. I interact with few people and those are mostly ones I hire; lawyers, accountants, cleaners. I have no shortage of money, living forever and investing wisely ensures funds will never be an issue. The government certainly doesn't complain. My taxes probably pay the salaries of the Prime Minister and all his underlings. The thought makes me grimace, not the amount of taxes, but thinking of politics and such. They don't interest me and for the most part only give me a headache.

The computer is up and running so I check my email accounts while sipping my syrup. Mostly spam but one email catches my attention and I chuckle while I read it. A history professor wishes to know my sources for a post I made on a forum concerning interactions between Vikings and the natives of what is now Newfoundland. I delete the email. My source is myself, however I can't exactly say so.

I almost wish I could, scholars would love to pick my brain if they knew of my origins. Even the little I remember is so much more than they have uncovered. I would of course, have much explaining to do. They might end up picking at my brain in the literal sense.

Not only am I the first and only of my kind, this strange kind of vampire, I am also the last of my people. Even though when I was human, I'd only been a halfbreed of my race. The two are of course entwined. What I am now is due, at least in part, to what I had been then.

My mother had been of the Beothuk people, my father a Viking. Yes, I did smile when proof of their early visits to North America finally became discovered not too long ago.

I do not know exactly how I came to be born. I do know the Vikings came and settled an area near my mother's band for a few years before they finally left again. Whether or not my mother had been in love with my father, or if she had been raped or traded her favors for trinkets, she never said.

I remember almost nothing of my childhood. My first memories are of living amongst our small band on the coast. The Vikings, my birth, were never discussed.

I also do not know if my mother tried to pass me off as a full blood. If so, this backfired as I grew older. Yes I had our people's dark hair and eyes, however adulthood brought features which also resembled the Vikings. I cannot say I had been shunned because of this, though I know my mother did occasionally suffer from it. However I was beautiful, no matter what blood ran in my veins. Perhaps I would have had a normal life had the Vikings not returned.

Those who came the second time were not as friendly. Our people fought, many were killed. Due to the season we did not want to leave. We could not defeat them and they would not leave us be. What are a people to do? Our belief system was very complex. We worshipped the sun and moon and had great belief in the Spirit World. We asked for help in ridding ourselves of the Vikings. Many rituals were performed and still we perished at their hands. In desperation the elders deemed a sacrifice necessary. Of course they meant me. Though I was afraid, I did go willingly. What they did, what happened to me, I can't really say. At some point early in the ritual I lost consciousness.

When I awoke I found myself buried alive. Or not alive, however you want to look at it. I assumed then, and perhaps I was even correct, that I had been possessed by one of the spirits. How else could it be I had grown so strong? Everything about me had improved; all my senses, I healed quickly and apparently could not die. Only darkness weakened me.

Of course it took me some time to figure all of this out, once I dug myself out of my grave and stopped screaming. I did not return to my people. I knew it would be seen as a bad omen.

Once I adapted, which my people had always been good at doing, I grew strong. I taught myself to use what had been granted to me by the Spirit World. I attacked the Vikings myself until the few who remained fled. I suppose we did have our pleas answered, just not in any way we had thought.

I left my people to wander the wilderness alone. My problems with darkness made having companions dangerous. I did not learn until recently the last of my people died in 1829 and we had become extinct.

Except for me.

But then again, I suppose I don't really count anymore. The loneliness of my situation overcomes me again.

Grimacing into my cup at the sudden melancholy such memories brought forth, I rubbed at my forehead. My fingers take me to a forum I posted to only a month before. On a good note my post wasn't ignored. On a bad note I received a lot of crazy responses. I read the one new one and let out a sigh. Another person who didn't believe me. I definitely needed some cheering up now.

I log onto Twitter. I could always find some nonsense there that would make me smile.

My first sappy story went over so well I just had to continue it. My mind works in mysterious ways, and soon I found myself spending hours doing research online about where my sappy vampire came from.

The history mentioned is based on actual facts (minus the magic and strange vampirism of course). The Beothuk (or Beothick, Beothuck etc) were a small group of aboriginal people who lived on the island of Newfoundland centuries ago. They are often referred to as Newfoundland's Red Ochre People. 'Beothuk' meant 'people' in their language. Their origins remain uncertain, though their culture is thought to have formed around 1500AD. The last known Beothuk, a woman named Shanawdithit, died in 1829 from tuberculosis and the people became officially extinct. As for the Vikings, recent archeological evidence has found settlements in Newfoundland in Beothuck territory. It has been proposed the Beothuk were the Skraelings mentioned in Viking Sagas and that the two people both traded and fought. Though there is much not known about them, I was able to find a number of interesting sites online which included some great information and was a truly interesting read. If you would like to more I recommend doing a Google search for Beothuk Indians.

Why You Should Always Wear Clean Underwear

by

Sean Hayden

Okay, I'll admit it. I was probably *way* too drunk to be driving, but in my defense I did try to call a cab. Not my fault it was Friday night and every cab within a three county radius was busy with the stupid UFO convention in Spokane. Who the hell would schedule a major event like that in Washington anyway? Hell, I even saw three people in the little country bar I decided to hole up in wearing little pointy prosthetic ear tips. Not your usual clientele at a bar called "Cocktails". I know, I know, real original, but I didn't name it. I just consumed a good portion of their stock.

After I dropped my keys for the fifteenth time, I finally managed to get the slippery lil' suckers into the way too tiny (and I swear it was moving) key hole on the side of my powder blue 1973 Mustang. Once the door was open I gave the car a little pat on the roof for letting me in, and slid into the contoured leather seats. They didn't come contoured, but since I've had the same damn car since I graduated high school, my butt fit perfectly into the Stan shaped hole. See, contoured. If I ever sold the damn thing, I'd put that in the classified ad.

I managed to get the key in the ignition on the first attempt so I assumed sobriety wasn't too far out in my future. I was relieved since I would be operating heavy machinery (the Mustang) and disappointed because I had spent a small fortune getting fershnickered. I hoped my buzz wouldn't wear off before I pulled up in front of my trailer. Yes trailer, I said trailer. Do you have a problem with mobile home owners? Anyway, the car started and I put her into reverse. I even managed to leave the parking lot of "Cocktails" without sideswiping any jacked up pickup trucks. I deserved a cookie.

The highway was deserted. Hell, at 2 o'clock in the morning, everything's deserted except the police stations and hospitals. I was drifting along from lane to lane listening to my 8-track of Journey (everything in the Stang is original), singing to myself when the deer jumped out in front of me. Okay, maybe he was there the whole time but it sure as shit *looked* like he jumped out in front of me. I slammed on the breaks and gave the wheel an involuntary jerk to the right. Instead of stopping, the car started spinning. You remember that scene in "Top Gun" when he went into a flat spin? Yep, it happens in mustangs too, but I didn't have a Goose killing ejection seat. I imagine I would have continued spinning for quite a while, and I remember wondering to myself what the record was, when my attempt was halted by that damn tree (which also jumped out of nowhere).

I came-to sitting in the passenger seat (I never wear my seat belt. I know, I'm stupid, but I'm also driving drunk here so get over it). I almost started crying when I saw that a tree had started growing spontaneously from my engine block. Well, that's what it looked like from my particular vantage point, but then I saw my engine block sitting in the driver's seat. Either I was drunker than I thought or I was one lucky sumbitch. I needed anther drink, and a lawyer. I wondered how long I had until my luck ran out and a Washington State Trooper drove by and saw how my car had been molested by the local flora.

I opened the damn door and raised my eyebrows in appreciation at how my car continued to cooperate even though it lie there a broken, bloody mess. I managed to struggle to my feet (no meager task even before the accident. They should give out medals to people with abilities such as mine) and backed away from my baby, seeing if there was any more damage than engine displacement and minor body repair. Maintaining a

31

positive outlook, I circled her once and made a silent Sign of the Cross. There, in the dim light of the moon, I gave my beautiful Mustang last rights and said my farewells.

The moonlight surrounding me kept building in intensity. In my less than sober state, I knew in my heart that God himself had sent a choir of angels to pay homage to such a wonderful feat of classical engineering and good ole American ingenuity. I sat silently waiting for their approach, never taking my eyes from my love, nor my hand from my heart. The light coalesced around me and I could feel its angelic properties as it warmed me from within. I could see the very molecules of my Stang start to shimmer. God was going to give my baby a place of honor within the hallowed halls of heaven. With any luck he'd make her a beautiful angel. She deserved it! I looked up and saw the tree shimmering as well. I hoped God was a car lover and sent that evil tree straight to the depths of hell!

Something was wrong. Everything around me was glimmering, too. It didn't stop there either. I could see the very molecules of everything around me losing whatever it was that held them together. Leaves and quarter panels broke apart into jumbled blobs of green and powder blue. I held up my hand and could only see a floating mass of peach colored grains of sand vaguely in the shape of a glove. With a clash of thunder and a burst of colors unimaginable to a mortal brain, the world around me exploded into nothing.

I awoke spread out on a cold metal table in nothing but my boxer shorts. Gasping for air, I lifted my arm and sighed in relief as I saw it once again was whole and not in a gazillion little specks.

I sat up, expecting to be lying in some room in a hospital. Sure, the room looked like it served some sort of medical purpose, but I knew it wasn't a local hospital or even one of those new emergi-centers. I started to shake as I knew in my heart I wasn't in Washington anymore, or even Kansas for that matter.

Everything was made of the same metal as the table and shone almost blue it was so black. I stood (still a little inebriated so I guess you could call it more of a sway) and glanced at the equipment that hadn't been made in Japan, let alone our world. At that moment I knew it wasn't angels that had come to pay their respects to my dying vehicle.

Behind me a door swooshed open and I heard sucking sounds. Spinning quickly I prepared to defend myself from the evil aliens and their all too familiar anal probes.

There in the doorway, stood exactly what I expected, an alien.

I immediately relaxed my posture. Nothing that cute could be dangerous. It looked like a hairy sea anemone but with those stupid little googly eyes that humans love to glue to everything. Rocks, notebooks, hell I even saw a pair glued to maracas once. I never got the fascination.

The alien moved forward, making little sucky noises with his feet.

"That would probably be handy in zero gravity," I thought as the little fellow reached over to a small table by the doorway and picked up what looked like a little metal ice cream cone. He held it out to me. I smiled and reached for it when the shaft of blue light struck me in the chest.

"Sonofabitch," I thought. "The little bastard tazed me." I expected to fall to the ground and flop around like a trout, but instead discovered I simply couldn't move. Not one muscle in my body was mine to command.

I watched helplessly and without even the ability to blink as the little alien walked over to me and placed a metal disk behind my ear. The door swooshed open again and a second alien joined the first.

"Have you installed the translator?"

"Yes, My Lord," the first alien said with a little bow. "He will make a beautiful addition to the Zagomorph Museum. Unlike the other specimens we have captured from this planet, this one managed not to soil his undergarments upon capture."

This is yet another of my S.H.I.T.S! I've always been a huge SCIFI buff, but I'd never written any before this story. I love the whole ideas of aliens flying around in their little spaceships, probing...er...I mean studying us from afar. Another thing that made this story special to me is everything I had ever written, even now, I've always LOVED the main character. In this story, not so much. He was sort of douchie from the beginning. It made it so much easier to write his museum-bound doom. What was ironic was he managed not to soil his underpants.

Echoes of Darkness

by

Jen Wylie

I am suffering. Slowly being torn apart, breaking.

There is nothing I can do. Nothing but simply watch my world crumble to pieces around me. Nothing but watch you slowly continue to change, becoming someone I don't know, someone full of such frightening darkness and hate.

As your Echo I am bound to you, compelled by magic to come when you call, to help and protect you. Since you stole me from death and made me what I am with your Immortal magics, I have had no choice in that. Once, it didn't matter. Once, I waited longingly for attention. I wanted to keep you safe.

I don't know when it started. They came so gradually I can't recall when the changes in you began. I do know the why. So many little things, and big things, have happened to turn you against the world. Against me. They weren't my fault, or yours. Things happen, as they tend to do. We can't control everything, even though we sometimes try. You can't stop trying now. Control and power has become everything to you and I have become…nothing.

Why won't you let me help you? I am nothing to you now, merely the Echo made centuries ago to do your bidding. Someone you cheated from death, who didn't want to die so accepted your cryptic assistance not knowing the price. I survived those first years of confusion. With your help I learned how to walk the real world and the Otherworld and became powerful. I made you stronger, protected you and fought the Echo's of your enemies. For you.

I grew to love you, and not because of the magic binding us. You were a good man then, shining, bright, beautiful and full of hope and love. Before the darkness descended upon you I had been more to you as well, almost the living human I once had been. I know you didn't love me, not like I loved you, but once you at least saw me as a person, not as the thing I have now become.

You were my beautiful Immortal, my creator, my master, my everything. There had been a time when your beautiful eyes looked upon me warmly, twinkling with laughter and happiness. Now they regard me coldly, so full of anger, rage, and darkness I am forced to look away. Once your hands had touched me gently, though you didn't love me, you had accepted my love. You had at least cared for me. I avoid those hands now. Rarely do I materialize into solid form around you now, not since they touched me with such violence, and mad fury.

I cannot bear the changes which have come over you. The hatred in your heart has driven you into madness, of that I am quite certain. I couldn't stop it. I don't know how to bring you back. This tears me apart, being unable to help you, being hated by you.

Leaving is not possible. I have considered it, each part of me warring against the other. It doesn't matter what I want though. I am bound to you, while you live, at your call I must always come. I could leave your side when I am not needed, at least in theory. Yet I have always been with you, always. I don't know how to live without you. I can't live without you. You have always been, and always will be, everything to me.

I don't know what to do.

I will not leave. Staying is destroying me.

I don't know what to do.

There is no choice in the end but to continue to suffer your cold eyes, your dark, wicked smiles. I will look away from the evil deeds you do, from the darkness you are bringing to the world. I will not stop you. I cannot stop you. Yet I will not help you either.

You know this, which is part of the reason you hate me. Still you use me as you can, I cannot prevent it. You made me this way when centuries ago you took my dying breath and bound me to you. I am immortal, but an echo of what you are, of the human I once was.

I am nothing. I am everything. I cannot die, yet am dying. Your darkness and hate are smothering me, destroying me.

I can only hope it will end soon, my agony, my dark despair. Someone, someday, will stop you. Your Immortal life will be extinguished. I will be free of you then. If I survive. If I don't give my life trying to save you from them. If I don't break apart into nothing first.

Until such a time comes I will stay always beside you, loving you, suffering, breaking apart. I do not doubt the agony of it all will eventually destroy me. Then again, perhaps you will one day tire of torturing me.

Perhaps you will destroy me yourself.

This flash story is part of my Immortal Echoes world. It is from the point of view of Rhea, the Echo of the Immortal Simon. They appear briefly in my short story The Untouchable Echo (coming spring 2012 from Echelon Press).

The Day I Got Caught

by

Sean Hayden

What can I say? I'm an asshole. I know what you're thinking and I agree, *knowing* is half the battle. Well, G.I. Joe be damned, being an asshole has worked for the first twenty-four years of my life, and I'm not about to change now. Nobody would, not when they've led the semi-charmed kind of life I've had.

It wasn't always this easy either. Being the only son of a pharmaceutical rep has both advantages and disadvantages. Free drugs, *yay*. Never seeing your father, *boo*. Mom ditched us when I was just a baby, so Gramma became a permanent fixture when I was little. Her death when I was seventeen damn near killed me. I'm not so sure it didn't drive me a little insane. Insane enough to start raiding Papa-san's goody bag on the rare occasion he graced me with his presence after Gramma's funeral. He pretty much left me alone after that with my very own credit card as my sole companion.

Yeah, that pretty much started the ball rolling on the moral declination avalanche that became my life. I did learn one thing though. There is such a thing as balance and everything in life *is* inversely proportional. As the "Fuck Yes My Life Rules" factor went up, my grades plummeted. The more fun I had, the less true friends I found myself hanging around with. The more I wanted to impress a girl, the less I did. Oh, well, I still wouldn't want to be anybody else but me.

I quickly became bored with everyone and everything around me. Until "The Day", as I like to refer to it. Without a doubt, the best thing that could ever happen to anybody in the world happened to me.

Sleep had pretty much eluded me the night before. Not an uncommon occurrence when Daddy Dearest was home. A good night's sleep was nothing compared to the pharmacopoeia roller-coaster I rode until I finally passed out around three. See, the old man had a top sales position for a pharmaceutical company that made most, if not all, of the specialty treatment drugs custom designed to alter brain functionality. How do I know this? My Daddy done told me so, several hundred times. Not to mention the liberal samplings I delved into on lonely Friday nights.

That morning (afternoon, whatever) I woke up with the fuzziest head you could imagine. I felt like somebody had stuffed cotton balls in my brain. I shook my head and tried to moisten my mouth with the half empty bottle of water sitting on my nightstand to clear it up. The tepid liquid did nothing to help. I was going to need something stronger. Something with a little more pep. Something that had enabled man to climb mountains, lift enormously large objects, build pyramids, jump over buildings, and reach the farthest depths of our universe: *coffee*.

God gaveth the coffee, I kill you if you taketh away. I'm having T-shirts made, order now.

I made my way into the kitchen and shoved a pod into the Keurig coffee maker. Happiness, brewed one cup at a time. Only Americans could find a better, faster way to perfect perfection. I watched the little "I'm green, you can enjoy your life again" LED flicker on, letting me know my coffee was ready. I sat at the little marble kitchenette table and sipped my mug of pressurized heated water slowly drizzled over the ground legumes of the Coffea arabica tree, and even that didn't help. My head was still fuzzy. Not fuzzy like in I just tried to take an eye exam after swimming in an over-chlorinated swimming pool. It was more of a I just downed a bottle of Nyquil feeling (yes, I am speaking from experience).

41

I heard footsteps behind me and turned to see the not too happy visage of my father walking into the kitchen.

"I need to talk to you, Jimmy," he said and leaned against the door frame of our all too small kitchen.

Images of him noticing missing pills in his bag, finding stashes of other non-pharmaceutical life enhancers in my room, and him noticing the movie titles of rented pay-per-views on the cable bill flashed before my eyes. I wondered not at what I had done; rather at what he had caught me doing.

"Do you know your credit card bill was over eight thousand dollars this month? How the hell do you expect me to keep financing your fun?" He came over to sit with me at the table.

I said the only thing I could at such a ridiculous revelation, "Umm, I don't know?"

"You graduated from high school over a year ago. It's time to grow up, son. I looked into it, Jimmy. With your academic achievements in high school and your current SAT scores, you could definitely have a well rounded career as either a carnival ride operator, or as a strip mall security professional."

I couldn't help it. I laughed *and* said, "Cool."

"This isn't funny, Jimmy. I got you a break though. As it turns out the Dean of Duke University's son was diagnosed with paranoid schizophrenia. I just happened to find this out and offered to get him on some drug trials for new medications, if he found a place for you in the hallowed halls of his university. You're starting at Duke next week. Congratulations."

"Fuck that, Dad," I said and managed to duck under his swinging open palm. At least he didn't punch me.

He didn't come around the table and beat the shit out of me like he wanted to (I could see it in his eyes). "Let me rephrase this then," he said calmly. "If you don't pack

42

your shit up and get your ass to the dorms at Duke, enroll in classes, and do exceptionally well, I'm going to cancel your credit card, report your car stolen, fill the fridge with hot-pockets, and let you live off that while I'm away on business. Do we have an understanding?"

"Clear as crystal, Dad." I sighed resignedly.

I saw the world (my world, my perfect, perfect world) crashing down around me. The fuzziness in my head didn't even fade. If anything, it felt worse than before. I could feel the world blackening around me, and I stared at my father's face. It wasn't moving. I heard something like a rush of water and the rest of the room came into focus. The fuzziness left and everything became clearer. My father still wasn't moving.

"Dad?" Still nothing. I held my hand up in front of his face and started waving it back and forth. Still nothing. I reached over, closing the last few inches between him, and poked him solidly in-between the eyes, fully expecting him to be fucking with me.

I gasped as my finger made contact with his skin. My father sired me in his later years. I think he was around thirty-five when I was born, and I used my rusty mental math skills to figure him to be around fifty-fourish. My father wasn't a skinny man, nor was he fat, but he did have excess skin on his face and brow which should be quite, pardon the expression, squishy.

He wasn't. His skin held the texture of stiff plastic. I stood from my seat. I grasped his hand in mine and slowly lifted his arm from the table. It was mobile, but barely.

The strangeness of it struck me. It wasn't heavy or difficult to move, his arm just moved slowly. I stepped back and kept walking backward, staring at my father until my tailbone collided with the kitchen counter. I stopped

43

and turned, finding the sink behind me. I reached down and lifted the faucet handle.

Nothing came out of the faucet. I lifted up and down on the handle. Just as I was ready to scream in frustration I looked closely at the tap. There was water coming out, but so slowly I could barely follow its progress. Water hung in a solid stream from it, but only about a half-an-inch long. Without thinking I reached down and touched it. It was wet, and cold, but it clung to my hand like some sort of plastic polymer instead of good old H20.

"What the fuck," I said and backed up again. This time I rammed into the table where my father sat.

Without thinking, I sat and stared at my father again. In the edges of my vision I could see the blackness that had been there when the fuzziness started. I looked at the face of the only person who had remained constant throughout my whole life and now didn't want me around. *What other reason would he have for sending me away to college?* He had more money than God. He could bitch about the credit card bills all he wanted. I knew the truth.

The sound of rushing water returned and my father said, "I said, do we have an understanding?"

"Yes?" *What had just happened?* Hearing running water again I glanced around the kitchen. I fully expected everything to freeze again, but then realized the kitchen sink was running. My heart sank.

"Did you leave the sink running this whole time?" Dad walked over to the sink and shut it off. "I didn't even hear it when I came in."

"I'm going to go pack, Dad." I stood zombie-like. I wanted to be alone and needed time to think.

"Good son, you go do that."

That was "The Day". The day I got my powers.

As it turned out, and please believe me when I say this is all pure speculation, I had the ability to slip out of time.

I didn't "stop" time, I merely became unaffected by it. Water ran, smells still smelled, bullets traveled (I know, I checked) and machinery still ran, albeit very, very slowly.

I did what my father asked, and packed my stuff for Duke University. I had no idea what to expect when I got there, but I found the entire experience quite enjoyable.

I decided to earn my own living in the field of computer sciences. It was the one thing I seemed to have a knack for, and as it so happened, I could take as long as I wanted on the exams and they were all open book. Okay, due to my new abilities all my exams were time limit free and open book, but nobody else needed to know that. Often I would wait until *almost* the end of the exam and wander around the room writing down the answers that other people had filled in. I told you before I was an asshole, but you didn't believe me.

Don't get me wrong, I wasn't going to let all this academia interfere with my social life and new found abilities. No way, no how. I still had my father's credit card and the dorm rooms surrounding mine were party central. Amazing how people didn't card you for kegs of beer when you flashed a platinum card in their face. Surely an underage youth wouldn't have one of those, right?

Anyway, it was probably that last party that sent my father into an epileptic rage causing him to call the credit card company to put a cap on my spending spree. Old people suck. The worst part about it was he didn't even tell me. I had already spent about two-grand when the card came up *declined*.

I called my old man and he let me know in no uncertain terms that he had implemented a limit on my spending, *and* that he was proud of my GPA. It was the only reason he hadn't cancelled the card completely.

His foresight in meddling with my financial freedom forced me to improvise. That very week I started using my powers for evil (Muhahaha).

I know what you're thinking, I robbed a bank. Nope, that would be way to cliché. Although the thought did cross my mind. I wanted to have fun.

I started a website. A website where the male persuasion could go and enjoy the candid beauty of a woman in precarious short skirt wearing positions. Yup, I started a porn site. You see I learned a valuable lesson one day in-between time. Anything I was holding when I slipped still worked in my little pocket of non-linear chronological excursions. Ergo camera's worked just fine.

Technically I wasn't doing anything wrong either. I never shot a woman's face in the picture, merely positioned myself for the most effective angle. I fully expected to win the Pulitzer any week now. The photos were beautiful, and it never ceased to surprise me how many young females went around in skirts sans panties. Tsk, tsk and shame on them.

Months later and the website was a complete success with millions of subscribers and a plethora of sponsors. Who said the Dotcom Era was dead?

Anyway, that's when I saw her.

Her name was Samantha and she sat in the seat next to me every Wednesday and Friday in my HTML class. She was beautiful and sexy and perfect in every way. She had long brown hair and the face of an angel that had me hooked from the moment I saw her. I knew I just had to have a picture of her.

I planned everything out and started taking my camera to class with me. After class I would follow her around until she made her way to her next class. I would have gotten the picture much sooner, but the weather took an unlucky change to cool and she started wearing jeans to class every day. It took nearly a month before I got it.

I will never forget the moment either. I followed her from class and she took a different route. I fell back far enough where she wouldn't see me as she made her way to the student parking lot. She reached into her purse and pushed a button and the tail lights on the silver Camry a few spaces from her blinked merrily as the trunk popped open. This was it. I stopped my forward progress and watched as she bent into the trunk and deposited her books. I slipped out of time.

She stood frozen in time as I closed the distance between us. She couldn't have been more perfectly posed if I had positioned her myself. Slowly, I crept into position, nearly lying on the parking lot pavement to get the shot I had only dreamed of.

I smiled when I saw her panties. Somehow I knew she wouldn't be going around without them.

I lifted the camera and focused, setting my finger on the button to capture her in all her glory. The view through the LCD was amazing and I could feel my heart start to beat faster. Faster and faster, and then it nearly exploded when her face appeared below her skirt.

"What are you doing?"

That was The Day I Got Caught.

When I saw the topic, I actually panicked a little. I'm somewhat of a deviant myself and I have been most of my life. The problem was I had no experience to draw from. "The Day I Got Caught," was new! I had never been caught before! What could I possibly write about? Then it hit me...

An Unexpected Echo

by

Jen Wylie

I sat at my desk, puttering at editing one of my books when he first appeared. He hadn't made a sound, yet I felt his presence behind me. I closed my eyes for a moment before looking over my shoulder.

"Yes?"

He didn't speak at first, though he cocked his head slightly to one side, regarding me thoughtfully. I imagine I looked quite the sight. It was late evening and I'd recently gotten out of the shower and into a pair of pink camo jammies (they were a gift!) and had a towel turban-style wrapping my wet, long brown hair.

He, on the other hand, caught my attention and held it. He was of course, beautiful. Men who appear suddenly in your room often are. Strangely enough, this happens to me now and then. I will admit he wasn't typical of the few I'd seen before. His black hair hung straight, not quite touching his broad shoulders. His eyes were very dark as I stared into them, trying to figure out if they were blue or brown. I couldn't decide. Perhaps they really were black. His features were exotic, leaving me unable to clearly identify his origins, a mix of something I thought, perhaps Asian and Middle Eastern and who knew what else.

It did not escape my notice he wore no shirt, only simple pants with slightly tattered edges. He wasn't wearing any shoes at all.

Eventually I was able to speak. "Can I help you?" I tried to ignore the blush which crept over my cheeks at his intense scrutiny. I hate blushing. Unfortunately I'm rather prone to it.

A faint smile slipped across his fine lips. "I need you to tell my story," he said.

Leaning back I closed my eyes, letting out a sharp irritated sigh. I didn't have time for this. I needed to finish this editing, and I had three other books to finish and...

"It is important to me, that you do so."

I opened my eyes to look at him again. "I don't really have the time."

He smiled a sad little smile and bowed his head slightly in my direction. "Very well."

"Oh fine," I muttered. I'm a sucker for sad little smiles, what can I say? "But just a short one. I'm not writing a whole book about you."

His smile grew, yet the sadness remained in his eyes. "Thank you."

Great, his was likely a sad depressing story. What ever happened to sunshine and rainbows and happy endings? I brought up a new page on my computer. "Alright. Let's hear it."

He stared at me for a moment before grabbing a chair and pulling it over. He took a seat gracefully, leaning forward, elbows on his knees. "You wish me to tell you now?"

I looked at the clock. Crap, it was after ten already. "We'll do a quick session, alright?"

He nodded and smiled again.

Placing my fingers on the keyboard I looked over my shoulder at him. "So, what's your story about?"

"What I am. How I died, or didn't I suppose," he answered.

I leaned back, removing my fingers from the keys. "You're not a vampire are you?" If so I was in trouble. Vampires were so overdone lately.

"No. I am an Echo." His eyes crinkled in amusement. "You have written about us before."

Staring at him in surprise, a smile came to my lips. Another Echo? Very well, I'd liked the last story I'd told

50

about one of them. They were interesting, to say the least. Then I wondered how he knew I had written about Cassandra. I hadn't posted the novella online. I'd barely mentioned it in fact. The Forgotten Echo had been picked up for publication by my publisher but few others had seen it. Someone would be getting a serious swat.

I waved my hand at him to continue. "Tell me about what you remember of your past, before you became an Echo." I figured his reply would be quick, if he had one at all. I recalled Echoes rarely remembered their living past, some struggled to remember even their names.

"I was born in Egypt," he began. "As to a date I'm not sure when. A very long time ago. My father was Egyptian, my mother a slave, from a long line of slaves."

My fingers danced over the keyboard. "So you were a slave as well?"

"Yes," he said, tilting his head in acknowledgement. "I served in a Temple, as my mother before me. Back then, I struggled to make something of myself, I did everything I could to please those above. In my zealousness to rise above what I had been born into, I angered one high official, overstepping my place. I was beaten and left to die outside the Temple grounds."

He spoke of his punishment with no feeling, but his words caused a painful, sad knot in my chest. Yet I didn't know quite how to respond, so just continued typing, giving him only a sympathetic glance. "Go on."

"Death eluded me for a time, my body and spirit fighting to live. However it was not to be. Before dawn I felt the battle was lost. I prepared myself for death."

He stopped and I looked back at him. He was staring off into nothing, perhaps recalling the moment. "But you didn't die," I prodded.

He nodded. "No. A woman appeared. She was beautiful, she was kind. She offered me life for servitude and I accepted. Kneeling next to me she placed her lips over mine and took my last breath." The small smile appeared again. "Looking back, I know I was lucky. Not only that she chose me, but because she stayed with me, and taught me about what I had become. An Echo, more than a ghost, a servant to an Immortal."

"Can you tell me about her?"

"Her name was Amunet. Like I said, she was beautiful, and also powerful. Not only politically, she was an Immortal, cursed or blessed to live forever and never age. She had powers normal people didn't. I stayed by her side for a long time, learning my powers, growing into them. I discovered how to walk in the Otherworld and this one, how to be almost human again."

I paused and turned around. "Wait, you said was. Her name *was* Amunet."

"She died…" He faltered. "She was killed only a few decades after she created me."

I opened my mouth and closed it again. Echos' protected and fought for their Immortals. If an Immortal was killed, it was usually after their Echo's had fallen.

"You're Unbound," I finally manage to say. "Or did another Immortal bind you to them?"

He shook his head. "You are correct. I am Unbound. I am free. Through much effort I have managed to stay so all these centuries. I wish to stay so." He grimaced slightly. "I hid, for a very long time. I avoided both Immortals and other Echo's until I deemed myself powerful enough to prevent an Immortal from binding me."

"That sounds…lonely."

He shrugged and looked away. "It was the price I paid for my freedom." With another small smile he looked back at me. "I am strong enough now I don't need to fear them. The last few centuries I have interacted with the Immortals more often. I even assist them when I can."

"I see," I said, though really I didn't. I regarded him a moment before turning back to the computer. "So, what's the story then? You want me to write about all of this? Or is there something else going on?"

"Other things," he answered evasively. "There has been quite a bit going on lately I think you may be interested in."

Nodding, I glanced at the clock again. "I think this is enough for now." I was about to save my notes and stopped. "You never told me your name!"

He stood and came to stand beside me. With one finger he typed out his name...

Soul.

I blinked, confused for a moment at the word he'd typed, and then I smiled. I liked it. His story would be a good tale, especially with a name like that for the main character. I opened my mouth to tell him so, but he'd already disappeared. Saving what I had written and shutting down my computer I kept looking over my shoulder. Was he still here, but I couldn't see him? Did he watch me from the Otherworld?

I began closing up the house for the night, my thoughts on Soul and what stories he would tell. My mind ran in circles. I doubted I'd get any sleep, but I would try. Stories and characters seemed to always run through my mind. Ideas came to me in the strangest of forms. This night had certainly been strange.

Climbing into bed it occurred to me I didn't know if my unexpected guest would play the Hero or the Villain in my tale to come.

Soul is another result of my mind running in crazy circles when I should be sleeping. While working on The

53

Forgotten Echo I mention Unbound Echo's so of course I needed to think that out, which led to the creation of a character who was one. Soul's creation didn't quite happen like it is written above...but it was close. He makes an appearance in The Untouchable Echo and will one day have a story of his own.

It's too Friggin' Hot for This

by

Sean Hayden

The day started out like any other mediocre day. Lord knows I had experienced enough of them to recognize one when I saw it. I woke up in my little crap-hole apartment outside the dusty Mojave, CA airport and drank a pot of coffee. When I found the dead spider at the bottom of my first cup, I should have called it a day and went back to bed. They're called *omens* for a reason, folks. I just neglected to heed the one staring me in the face, literally.

I tossed the cup into the sink, got a somewhat clean one out of the cupboard and poured myself another cup. I know what you're thinking, "If you live in a friggin' desert, why would you drink coffee?" The answer is quite simple. Could you fly an airplane four hours south into the heart of Mexico and then four hours back without it? The answer is no and neither could I.

I took my second cup of coffee and stepped out onto the little patio balcony every apartment at the "Sandy Ridge" apartment complex had. The sun had been up for an hour already and stepping outside was like taking a stroll through a blast furnace.

"It's too friggin' hot for this," I mumbled and stepped back into the more moderate temperatures of my apartment. I finished my coffee and donned my usual khaki pants and (used to be) white tank top. I slipped my boots on my feet without bothering to lace them up and put my aviator sunglasses on my face. I bought them in the eighties when "Top Gun" came out and I had a legitimate job as an airline pilot. I thought they made me look like Tom Cruise. Getting fired from the airline for "Flying while intoxicated" made me look like Tom Arnold. To say living in the desert and drinking my dinner every night made me look old was probably something of an understatement.

The ride to the airport was an unbelievably short one. If it weren't pushing 110F outside I could walk to my sturdy little Cessna 172. As it was, I could barely stand the walk between my apartment and the car. One time, as a joke, I had cracked an egg over the pavement of our dilapidated parking lot. It cooked. It cooked fast. Just wish I could afford bacon.

I made my way to where my little plane was parked and stood under the wing to catch my breath. In the shade it wasn't too bad. As I looked back at the main concourse for our tiny airport, it looked submerged under water from the heat vapors coming off the Tarmac.

"It's too friggin' hot for this," I mumbled and stepped into the blistering heat of the sun to unlock the door to the cockpit.

I did a quick pre-flight check, anxious to get underway. Without so much as a second glance at my instruments, I started the engine and radioed the tower for clearance.

"See you back here tonight, Wayne, and stay outta trouble in Mexico," Jimmy radioed back from the air-conditioned tower.

See, my trips to Mexico were to pick up anything that was being shipped by my current employer. Sometimes it was artifacts he sold off to local museums, sometimes it was cheaply made designer knock offs, sometimes it was drugs. It was whatever he could get his hands on down there and bring back here. It was never legal. Jimmy in the tower knew this, and was probably paid more than I was, just to keep his mouth shut.

The plane started and I taxied over to the main runway. A little goose of the throttle and I sped down the runway at takeoff speed. I could feel the exact moment the tires left the safety of the ground in the pit of my stomach.

I was about a hundred feet off the ground when the spider crawled across the dashboard of my single engine plane. I was about a hundred and fifty feet when the spider stopped and turned to gaze curiously at the human with both hands on the wheel. At about two-hundred feet, I'd just about had enough of the spider and let go of the controls with my right hand to give the creature a swat he'd never forget. Just before the palm of death delivered the final blow, the engine blew.

I heard the boom and grabbed the controls of my small plane. The only thing I could see was black smoke. It rolled greasily over the glass and hung there forming little droplets. I must have thrown a rod. The second boom came and I heard a large tearing noise. It sounded horribly like a propeller shredding metal, but I still couldn't see anything because of the smoke. My instruments started blaring and beeping at me. Mercifully the smoke cleared. Just long enough for me to see the ground before the nose of the plane smashed into it.

I woke, relatively unscathed from my ordeal, and pushed myself through the busted windshield. I kicked the front of the plane and spat curses at it about its mother as I turned to get my bearings.

The runway of the Mojave airport faced north, so I always had to turn a full one-hundred and eighty degrees before heading down to Mexico. I hadn't even started my turn when the engine failed, so I was probably somewhere in the southern regions of the desert. I needed to get back to the airport before I got eaten by something or died of dehydration. Surely they would be sending out rescue vehicles shortly, right?

Maybe my radio still worked! I got down on my knees, stuck my hand back through the windshield, and felt

58

around for the handset to my radio. I really didn't want to have to climb back in through the windshield, but I couldn't find it. With a resigned sigh, I stuck the upper half of my body in and hit my head against the roof when I saw my body still harnessed into the cockpit chair. White as a ghost (literally), I backed out the way I had come and stood in the middle of the desert staring at my broken plane (and body).

"What the hell?" I had just finished speaking when the pit opened up beneath me.

"Exactly," something said behind me as I started to fall.

I can't even tell you how long I fell. It's impossible to measure time while you're screaming. The walls of the pit were made of molten rock that gave off little puffs of black smoke as they momentarily solidified and then re-melted. I could smell fire, and brimstone, and burning flesh wafting up the tunnel as I sped toward my destination.

I had no illusions. I knew exactly where I was headed. I hadn't led the most saintly of lives and I had always known I needed to repent and clean up my life. I just had never gotten around to it. Oops. Surely this was a mistake. Surely I hadn't led that bad of a life, right? I'd never killed anyone. I had slept with a couple of married women, but that was their fault! Not like I made a habit of it at any rate. By the time I hit the bottom, I'd realized and accepted my fate.

Since I was dead, the fall didn't kill me, but it hurt like a sonofabitch. I looked around and saw I was in a cavern filled with sad looking and dazed ghosts just like me. They all headed in one direction like they were being pulled toward something. Some of them were kicking and screaming and sliding over the hot coals that covered the entire floor of the cavern.

I couldn't understand why they would be burning their bodies rather than just going with the flow of the rest of eternity's shades. I felt a tug in my chest pulling me as well, gave a little sigh, and walked toward my fate.

I found myself in another line. This one was longer than the one at the D.M.V, and yet seemed a little happier. I always knew there would be lines in hell. I tried to talk to the other souls around me, but every time I opened my mouth to speak, fire would pour from my throat and burn my mouth. After the second try, I stopped. That's me, Mr. Quicklearner.

I sat in the line for hours, maybe days, who knows? Finally I could see a tall man in black robes standing at a podium made of bone. He stared at the people before him, but I couldn't hear him saying anything. Suddenly he would raise his arm, and they would pass to whatever was behind him. Most of them started to bawl uncontrollably.

Finally I stood before him. I say "him", but it wasn't a person. I could see a skeletal face inside the hood of the black robe, and I knew I finally had met Death. For some reason I always had it in my mind that Death would be a woman. I was screwed, but I decided to show some dignity as I faced him. I puffed up my chest and strode forward.

"Wayne Richards, you have led a life of frivolity and greed and never once have you ever had one concern for your fellow man. You are hereby sentenced to an eternity in the fiery pits of hell."

"Great," I couldn't help but mutter.

"Know this," Death continued. "You have three chances to pick your fate. I give you this warning, should you not resign yourself to either of the first two torments, the third will be filled with unimaginable horrors and torments, so choose wisely."

I nodded to Death and walked forward.

I stepped past and found myself back in the desert. Hell (and I use the term lightly), I could even have been back in the Mojave. The only thing different was the size of everything. We had the same species of cacti, but the ones before me were gigantic. I could feel the heat of the sun cooking me from the inside out, so I scrambled forward to find shade. It was then I noticed my hands. Gone were my normal hands and in their place were black pincers like a crab. My arms were shiny, black, and encased in chitin, too. I looked back at my body and I saw I wasn't human at all. Death had made me a scorpion.

I could feel the heat of the sand literally cooking me. I remember reading that scorpions had to hide during the day or be boiled in their own fluids, so I scrambled for a rock or anything to hide under.

I bet you can guess how quickly a two inch scorpion can move over hot sand. Yep, I looked like friggin' Speedy Gonzales, but I couldn't find a rock or anything. I could feel my insides start to burn as I dragged over the sand looking for shade. I knew hell was going to suck, but this was ridiculous. I was going to die (again) before I found safety. I crawled for hours and yet I didn't die. The only thing I knew was pain.

"It's too friggin' hot for this," I mumbled through my tiny scorpion mouth.

The desert around me vanished.

I came to on a grassy tundra. Glancing around showed me I was completely surrounded by tall grass and not one tree. I quickly looked down at my body and saw I wasn't a scorpion anymore, instead I had the body of a lion. Death had sent me to Africa. I could do this! All I needed was to find some water and a cave. I should have wished for a feather bed and a six pack of beer. For days I wandered through the scorching heat, determined to spend the rest of my days as a lion. At night the sun would go

61

down and offer a reprieve, but by then I was too exhausted to move. Slowly I crept through the grass, trying to find something to quench my thirst and offer me protection from the sun. I truly knew hell.

On the third day, I gave up and rolled over onto my lion back and gave up. I could feel the sun burning me through my fur, and there wasn't anything I could do. I tried to suffer through the pain, but again, just like before, I couldn't die. Night came and went and for days I waited on the verge of death.

"It's too friggin' hot for this," I rumbled through my lion's mouth.

The grassy plain faded away.

I woke, lying next to a highway. Cars sped by me without even noticing. I was still too drained from my ordeals to even move. The heat around me was unbearable. If that wasn't bad enough, the humidity in the air made it impossible to breathe. Death was right. My third eternity would be the worst. I crawled forward and saw a metal post in front of me. I looked up and saw...

Welcome to FLORIDA
The Sunshine State

I live in Florida and have a job that requires me to be outside some days. It's not too bad in the winter-time, but come July... Yeah, it's like working on the surface of the sun, in 100% humidity. Well, I tend to bitch about the heat on twitter a lot. One of my friends suggested writing a story about it. This was the end result!

The Smallest Maestro

by

Jen Wylie

I am but a simple cricket.

No, not so simple. I am in fact a maestro of the simple tones, of perfect, joyful repetition. I can play in harmony or become the lone sound in a silent night.

Tonight the silence is deafening. The burning need to play overwhelms me. I begin, first testing the sound in delicate chirps before bursting into my constant tune. Over and over I relentlessly play; bringing sound to the silence, joy to all those who hear. My repeating notes echo beautifully in the darkness.

A sound disrupts me, a harsh human word, and I pause. Thumping, banging and anger filled tones shake the air, make the very ground beneath me tremble.

Suddenly everything is silent once more, and again I begin to play. The glorious sounds I make break the quiet, shattering it into delicious sounds which certainly delight every ear. For hours I play and certainly those are moans of pleasure I hear even from the humans who act so high and mighty.

Their moaning stops and again the noise of human speech drowns out my song. "WHERE THE HELL IS IT?"

I continue to serenade them, to attempt to lull them again into blissful sleep.

The ground shakes with each footstep, and yet I miss not a note. The air resounds with words I cannot comprehend and so I play louder, more desperately, more joyfully.

Sudden light startles me and my playing ceases as instinct causes me to freeze. But it is nothing, nothing but a mere human who cannot even make such joyful sounds. I begin to play again to share my–

Splat!

"GOT HIM!"

The Smallest Maestro

This little short is dedicated to every person ever kept up in the night by pesky crickets. I'm one of those people who wake up at any little noise. Summer nights when the crickets are singing so loudly earplugs don't even help are the bane of my existence. I often wish my bed was enclosed in a little soundproofed bubble. Yup, that would be cool.

The Headless Norseman

by

Sean Hayden

"Will you hurry up, Vern?"

Vern glanced over at his buddy Earl sitting in the prow of the tiny fishing boat the two had bought together thirty years ago. The pristine white paint had faded long ago and recently started pulling away in strips. The two had been fighting for two weeks over who had the responsibility of dragging it up to the boathouse, sanding it, and repainting it. Neither wanted to do it. "Hurry up with what?"

Earl smiled at his long time friend and said, "Losing. Biggest fish wins. So far I'm kicking your butt. Not that it's hard when all you catchin' is bait."

"Oh, shut up. I expect the winning fishy here in a moment."

"Suit yourself, but the fog's rollin' in."

Vern glanced out of the tiny bay they often frequented and gasped. They lived in Maine, and fog was a common occurrence, but the sheet of white rolling in was thicker than Vern had ever seen. "You win, let's go."

Earl started cackling with glee. *In an hour we'll be in Tompampka tavern sippin' suds and tellin' fish stories.* He grabbed the oars and started rowing while Vern brought in his line. Before it got even halfway in, the big spinner reel started screaming like Earl's ex-wife when she caught him with her sister. He stopped rowing, figuring Vern had gotten snagged on an abandoned lobster trap.

The boat stopped. The line didn't.

"What the hell you got, Vern?"

"Beats the hell out of me. Line's gonna snap in a second."

As soon as he said it, the line stopped. It didn't snap, it just stopped spinning.

67

Vern tentatively started reeling in again. The tip of the pole bent down and nearly touched the water. "It's big whatever it is," he told his friend clutching the oars.

Maybe he was wrong. Maybe he did snag something. Whatever it was he was slowly reeling it in. It didn't fight or pull, it was just heavy.

"Damn lobster traps," Earl muttered behind him.

The line got shorter and both of them leaned over the side of the boat waiting in anticipation. The line started moving back and forth and they leaned back a hair, thinking maybe it was just a tired fish. When the barnacle covered orange safety cone broke the surface of the relatively calm ocean, they both started laughing hysterically. That would be a tale for the bar tonight.

Vern set his pole in the boat while Earl rowed them into the fog. They needed to skirt the coast for two small coves before they would hit the docks.

Vern flipped the switch on the battery powered lantern they kept for foggy conditions. Usually it penetrated the darkness easily. This time, with the fog as thick as it was, all it did was cast an iridescent globe around their boat.

"Damn, it's foggy," Vern said.

"Better than rainy, come on. Let's hurry up."

"What's the matter, Earl. Afraid the Headless Norseman is gonna getcha?"

"It's the headless horseman, you twit."

"Nah. I meant what I said. The Headless Norseman."

Earl rowed in complete silence for twenty whole seconds before he took the bait. "I give up. What's a Headless Norseman?"

"Oh, come on. Everyone knows that tale! Leif Ericson? Ring a bell?"

"What the hell you talking about, Vern? Every dimwit in the country knows Leif Ericson landed in Canada! New Foundland as a matter of fact!" Vern could hear the pride in Earl's voice when he pulled the little known factoid out of his ass.

"Yes they do, and yes he did. What most people don't know is he returned to Finland to be a courtesan or something or other to the king. The king who ordered him to find more new lands. That's when he landed in Maine. That's when he was cursed by Penobscot's Medicine Man."

Earl gulped. Everyone knew the area they lived in was once the lands of the Penobscot Indians. There were few things Earl knew less about than Native American heritage. "Medicine man?"

"Yeah. Ole' Leafy-boy thought he would claim this land for the king, too! Killing the Norseman wasn't good enough for the Medicine Man. He had to curse him for good measure. 'To wander all eternally, headless' is how the curse goes I believe."

Earl gulped in foggy air. "W-w-what does that have to do with us?"

"Well, you see. Leif wasn't a dumb Sweed. He wandered headless for years and then he figgered out that if he cut off someone *else's* head and put it on his shoulders he could use that head to eat, see, and breathe for the night. It's a good thing he doesn't find his way to the coast more often. There would be a *lot* of headless corpses in the area."

"Find his way to the c-c-coast?"

"Yeah. You see he set sail on his ship and took the heads of all his men, since they let him get killed. Now they share in his torture. Must be tough to row when you're a stump, know what I mean?"

69

Earl gulped again and nodded. Vern's story was bothering him more than he liked to admit.

"Yeah, he comes back every so often. When he gets hungry."

Vern didn't say another word as he rowed. Both men strained to see the shore. They should be reaching the docks any moment, but neither could see. Anything.

"Where the hell is it?" Earl sounded close to panic and Vern gave a soft chuckle.

"Relax, scaredy cat. We should be there any second. As a matter of fact, there it is!" Vern pointed to the lights on the dock posts about five hundred feet away.

"Thank God!"

Earl seemed to be trying out for the Olympic Rowing Team. Vern thought about jumping out and water-skiing back to the dock. He laughed. *Maybe he shouldn't have told Earl that old story...*

The docks grew closer and Earl slowed his frantic rowing, huffing and puffing as he sat there while the dock lights became brighter and brighter. He set the oars to and turned to grab the well worn pylons and tie them off. It took a few moments for him to notice something wasn't right. The lights were up too high, well above where they should be. It wasn't until the small fishing boat collided with the ancient Viking warship that Vern and Earl realized what was going on.

When the Viking landed in the middle of the boat wielding a large, dented and rusted sword they screamed. When they looked up and saw the tattered remnants of his neck and the empty hollow above his shoulders they fainted.

They never woke.

The tiny fishing boat with the pristine white paint that had faded long ago, and recently started pulling away in strips, broke free from the icy autumn waters of the Atlantic. The cable that pulled it above the waves and held it there didn't even strain under the weight of the small boat. Sheriff Cobbs stood by the trawler arm of the Tugboat McGee next to the captain himself.

"Yeah, that's Vern and Earl's boat. Mystery solved. Drunk bastards probably fell overboard," the sheriff said disgustedly.

"Shame. They both owed me a beer," Captain McGee said wistfully as he swung the arm of the crane over the back of his tug. He slowly lowered the boat to the deck and unhooked the grapple hook. "Let's just hope Old Leif isn't back," he said
with a wink at the Sheriff.

"Oh, don't you be starting *that* story again."

I love Halloween. It is hands-down my favorite time of year and my favorite holiday. I love the candy, I love the costumes, I love the spookiness of it all. I especially *love carving me some punkins with my kids. We race through the store and find the newest punkin carvin' kits, with the latest designs and go to town. I top those off with one barfing punkin, perched on a table, spewing its innards onto the ground! When Halloween comes around, it really sets my creative juices flowing. I had never seen the Johnny Depp remake of* Sleepy Hollow. *I finally had an opportunity to watch it and was amazed. I truly loved it. As I laid my head down to sleep, The Headless Norseman entered my dreams...*

It Was a Dark and Stormy Night

by

Jen Wylie

It Was a Dark and Stormy Night

It was a dark and stormy night as I walked toward his cottage. I love rainy nights.

I waited at the wooden door a moment, listening for him. He too heard the rain and the wind and thought the elements, or maybe even God, was angry. *Silly man.*

I opened the door, surprising him slightly. He knelt, chilled and fumbling with the flint, by the fireplace. I could feel his eyes on me, and my dripping clothes, so I removed my cloak to please him. He smiled as I came forward and lit the fire for him. It blazed to life, warming us both.

He watched me hungrily, as I had watched him in town for many weeks. I had first seen him at a festival and noticed his interest in me. Being newly moved to the area, and living far from town, I hadn't seen him very much. What I had seen, and the stories I'd heard, was enough.

He was handsome and not all that old. He had nice teeth and hands not hardened by course labor.

I sat and beckoned him closer, not saying a word. I was beautiful, as I always was, pale skin and golden hair. He would come to me willingly. They always did.

He was surprised I had come, so I pulled him to me and professed my love. "I love you. I had to come, I couldn't stay away. Please forgive my forwardness. My love for you is so strong I couldn't help myself." I went on and on for a while, spewing out what he wanted to hear.

A small smile washed across his lips. He thought me week and in love like a mindless fool. But oh, his passion! To keep me for himself, always and forever.

"My fairest one, will you be mine?"

"But of course," I murmured, allowing him to pull my lips to his. Our kisses turned to more and I will admit I was surprised at his aptitude. Certainly I did not complain. He remained quiet, which often was his way. My lips quickly silenced any words I knew he was about to speak.

I dislike it when they talk.

Resting on fur rugs by the fire I watched his thoughts. His simple mind grew agitated and twisted, believing I was his, and then assuming I might leave for another.

Taking his face into my hands I stared into his eyes, and into his heart and soul. I saw what was there, and couldn't help but smile upon him. *Such twisted thoughts.* I was happy and proud to have found one such as him, alone with no kin or friends, two wives in the grave by his own hand.

I knew what he would do before he did it. I let him, without fighting or screaming. What could his soft hands about my neck do? I closed my eyes and lie still. Let him think me dead for now.

He lifted one of my lids and my eyes laughed, how beautiful a blue he thought. *Blue indeed! Was he color blind? They were green!* It was all I could do to keep from laughing aloud.

He thought me dead, and wondered at my blushed face. I am always rather pale but a little rouge can do wonders you know. Sadly it still shows when you're playing at dead.

I was growing tired of the game, so I merely rested and listened to his scattered thoughts. No, I would not stir a while yet. The best games took time, they couldn't be rushed.

Never once did he wonder what to do with me, or who might miss me. Leaving me dead on the floor he went about his evening chores.

I was delightfully surprised when he did not return to his bed, but settled down next to me, his thoughts now on how peaceful I looked in sleep. His arms wrapped around me, holding me close, and soon my killer fell asleep.

I listened to his heartbeat for a time, such a wonderful, tantalizing sound it was. Finally I removed myself from his embrace and brought him into mine. Ah! To see the surprise on his face!

I whispered to him, "God will not welcome one such as you. Why, you didn't even marry me first! See you in Hell, he who would kill one such as me! I will not be yours. I will not die." I smiled at his shock-wide eyes. "You, however…well that is another matter entirely."

My teeth ripped through his neck. He fought, but his strength was no match for mine. I fed until a true blush returned to my cheeks and my body hummed with power and warmth. I gave him one last kiss, and then donned my dry cloak and shawl. The rain had stopped, which brought another smile to my face.

I supposed you could say that the fire was an accident. I didn't mean to pour the oil over the bed and tip a candle. It's not my fault woods burns. Besides, it wasn't exactly a palace of a place.

The night outside was brisk and clear with just enough wind to fan the growing flames. I wiped my lips with my sleeve. Merely a drop of red.

The stars had not moved too far along the night sky and I smiled up at them, baring my lovely pointed teeth to the world. You see it was long till dawn, and the town was not far. Playing the game, it had been such a long time since I ate. A nibble here and there would eventually satisfy me.

I was soon gone from that little place. No one even knew I'd been there. No one saw me come or go. It is said the night embraces those such as I, a Child of Darkness.

75

"So tell me, my love, would you like a good-night kiss?"

This story was written a very long time ago 'when I was young'. As in a teenager. Even though I've never published a vampire story before, you'll see in this anthology I do have a soft spot for them.

And You Think Your Job Sucks

by

Sean Hayden

We're all guilty of it. Someone in the office steals our fucking box of paperclips and we turn into a snarling hateful ball of fury. If someone handed us a knife we would gladly slit the throats of the persons in the 8 cubicles surrounding us just to find the guilty party. We would paint our exposed flesh in their blood and dance on their bodies if decorum allowed. This is paperclips people. I'm not talking thumb tacks here.

Well, by day I work as a fiber-optic engineer (I can hear you saying what the hell is that, by the way). I've often had people ask me that. Basically I draw pretty maps with really cool Autocad software. See, I work for (duh duh duuuuuh) the cable company. The one I work for is a little different from the company hell bent on world domination by bringing you substandard programming at higher than normal costs. See the company I work for does fiber to the home. That means each house gets its own fiber for blazing fast internet, cable, and phone. Blah blah blah. My other job is I get to splice all the fiber with a really cool $22,000 piece of equipment. Outside. In Florida. Under the sun. I'm planning on moving the company to the surface of Mercury where it's cooler.

So, working outside in the middle of July in Florida sucks. I often bitch about my job. Then one day that all changed. Now I'm not going to sit here and tell you a tale of desperation. Nor am I ungrateful to be working. I realized from the get go that I'm one of the lucky ones who *has* a job in this economy. See, the guy who changed my outlook on today's modern workforce criteria and expectations was named Tom. Tom is one unlucky sonofabitch. Who's Tom? I'll tell you.

And You Think your Job Sucks

Believe it or not this whole tale starts with my son's underpants. He was 7 or 8 at the time and let's just say, he wasn't the best "wiper" in the world. We actually went so far as to call him, "Skidmarks," for a few days, hoping to embarrass him into being a little more "thorough" (if you know what I mean). I mean trying to break a kid of 8 whose philosophy has always been, "Wipe twice and get on with your life," wasn't easy. But we did it. Much to our dismay. Most of my hard earned salary went to the Charmin Corporation. The kid would use a roll each time he had a movement. We went through a twelve-pack a day. We were broke, but his ass was clean, and our sewer thingy out front of the house took a shit (pun intended).

The sewer thingy is basically a hundred gallon drum buried in the front yard which holds something called a grinding pump. Ominous sounding isn't it? It is. Basically it grinds up the poop and paper and then pumps it out into the sewer lines. *Nummy.* It worked perfectly until inundated with torrents of sheets of wadded up Charmin Ultra Soft, non-quilted, unscented (prior to use) death. My son killed the grinding pump.

I called the utility company. They sent Tom. Poor bastard.

Tom stepped out of the truck and could see water and unsavories escaping from the bolted down lid of the sewer thingy.

"Looks like you got a problem," he said.

"No shit," I replied and giggled at my charming witticism I was sure Tom had never heard before.

Tom grabbed a big ass (amazing how many puns I throwing in here ain't it?) toolbox and walked through the sloshy, stinky grass. Tom knelt down (yeah, in the grass) and drew out a 7/16ths ratchet and began unscrewing the lid. With each quarter turn of the tool, the smell intensified.

79

By the time he lifted the lid off I was gagging and horrified.

"You guys have spaghetti last night?"

Now I had heard dogs sniff the butts of other dogs to see what they had for dinner. Tom was just fucking amazing, it smelled like poop to me. But then I saw the noodles floating on the top of the brown muck. I must have forgotten to run the garbage disposal when I did the dishes. "Yeah," I replied embarrassed.

He nodded and opened the breaker panel. He flipped the switch a few times and sighed. "Looks like your grinder pump is shot. I'll have to replace it."

I looked down over his shoulder. "Where is it?"

He nodded at the drum of crap. "At the bottom."

Horrified I turned away. "How do you get it out?" I was afraid to ask.

"Well, I gotta reach down in there and grab it. Unless you wanna do it?" He laughed at his own joke. I cried.

"I'm good, Tom. You want a beer first?"

"Naw, I do this several times a day. You get used to it."

"Suuure you do. I'll be standing over there. Downwind. Let me know if you need anything," I replied.

"Fair 'nuff. Let me get some gloves." He reached into his tool box and brought out a box labeled "Latex Gloves". I would have kept looking until I found a box labeled "Latex Body Suits" but he seemed satisfied.

I'll be honest. You ever see the gloves the vets use when working on a cow's ass? You know the ones. They pull them on and then they stretch up to their shoulder? "Dig Deep, Daniel-san" gloves? I fully expected Tom to put one on. He didn't. He snapped on a little tiny glove and shoved his arm into the poop infested water up to his shoulder.

"Why did you bother?!" I screamed and ran around in horrified little circles.

"Bother with what?"

"Putting on the glove! Your shirt is in the fucking water!"

"I have another shirt in the truck."

"Do you have a shower?"

"No, but I have all my shots."

"Oh, good," I said and fainted.

Well, when I woke up, Tom had finished. He used my hose to rinse off his arm and went on his merry way. So next time you bitch about your job, I hope you remember my story of Tom, who truly has the shittiest job in the world (Ha! Another pun!).

I'm going to let you in on a little secret. Ninety-five percent of this story is based upon actual events. I'm not going to clarify which was fake and which was real. That will give you something to think about. NO, I didn't run around in circles, screaming like a little girl (MUCH). But I definitely didn't faint! I will say this. It was one of the most horrific things I've ever witnessed. I mean little gloves? WTF?

Forgettable
The Beginning

by

Jen Wylie

People forget things all the time. It's not uncommon. Every once in a while it gets you into trouble, but usually nothing too severe. For me forgetting is a daily occurrence, though not in the way you would think. My life has not been easy. Some parts were downright nasty and horrible. Some days are still bad, but things are getting better now.

Everything has a beginning, but sometimes, even looking back, it's hard to find. Different points could be considered the 'true' one. Once I forgot my favorite doll somewhere. I couldn't remember where, which was part of the problem. I was distraught for days and inconsolable. My parents did their best, but losing Miss Annie was a terrible blow to a five year old. Sometimes I think that was the start of it all... Even at such a young age the incident scarred me and made me paranoid about forgetting things. Whether or not this had anything to do with what happened when I was ten, I still don't know. Perhaps I never will.

I sat snuggled on the couch watching my favorite movie. It was late Saturday afternoon and the only cartoons on were stupid ones I didn't want to watch. The Guide told me it would be a few hours before one of my favorite shows would be on again. Luckily I knew how to work the DVD player, which was more than I could say for *Mom*, she didn't even know how to turn it on.

Duckie, my most favorite stuffie ever, sat propped up on the coffee table guarding my half-empty bowl of cereal that had been my lunch. He had replaced my favorite doll, Miss Annie, years ago and never left my side. Well, at school I had to leave him in my backpack, but he was still with me. Once he had been white but was now a faded grey color. He had a sparse fluff on the top of his head and dull orange beak. When I first got him, he had a thing inside that quacked when you pressed it. It stopped working after the fourth time Mom ran him through the washing machine. Even as worn as he was, he remained my favorite.

"Savannah! Time to get dressed! Savannah!" Mom popped her head into the room. "I've been calling you."

I couldn't tear my eyes from the TV, the good part was coming.

"We're going to be late, let's go!"

I did look up then. I had no idea we were going anywhere. Mom was dressed already. Not only that, she was dressed *up*.

"Hurry up! I put clothes on your bed."

I stared after her as she hurried down the hall. Grabbing Duckie, and with a few grumbles, I backed out of the room, still watching my movie.

"Turn if *off*! Come on, let's go!"

Doing as I was told, I trudged to my room. My nose wrinkled at the dress on my bed. I hated dresses.

Mom was digging in my closet. "Clothes. On now. I'll find your shoes. Teeth next." She looked over her should. "Quickly, please!"

"Where are we going?" I shrugged out of my jammies, leaving them on the floor, and picked up the dress. It was black with a strip of shiny red cloth around the waist. At least it wasn't too girly.

"Out. I have to go somewhere and your father was supposed to watch you, but now he isn't," Mom snapped. I didn't ask again. "Put on clean underwear."

Mom was looking angry by the time we made it to the car, so I sat quietly in the back, Duckie held firmly in my lap.

I wanted to ask where Dad was, and where we were going. I had a million questions but Mom's muttering and whispered curses as she drove through traffic kept my mouth shut. It was a long drive, and the city traffic was horrible. I watched the frustrated people in the cars next to us to pass the time.

For a while I'd known something was going on. They fought a lot. They didn't seem mad at each other, so I was pretty sure they weren't getting a divorce. It was something else. The phone rang a lot more than normal, too. When I was around they spoke quietly, or not at all. When I asked what was wrong, they just said it was "grown-up stuff" and not to worry. I tried not to, but still did sometimes.

Mom finally pulled into a parking lot and laughed when she found a spot right by the door. She cursed at the time, which read 4:34 on the radio display.

We got out and I studied the building and big sign on the side while she smoothed her skirt and locked up. Jameson Funeral Home. I knew a funeral was what you went to when someone died but I'd never been to one. *Had someone been sick and they'd died? Was that what had been going on? "Why are we here?"*

Mom ushered me toward the door. "I have to pay my respects and talk to some people. We won't be long."

"Who died?"

"No one you know. Just stay out of the way."

"Okay," I mumbled. The doors opened into a large waiting room with a lot of fake plants, flowers, and floral furniture. There were little pedestals with books on them around the walls. Signs above said a person's name and 'guestbook'. A long desk was off to the right with an older blond woman sitting behind it looking bored. A few old people sat quietly in chairs. One lady was crying.

Mom walked straight ahead, pausing by a tall, framed sign with a long list of names and room numbers. After a moment she continued down the hall and I followed quickly behind her. Muted voices whispered nonsense from all the open doors.

She turned into a room and stopped, pulling me off to the side. "I won't be long. There is a table over in the corner. You can have some cookies or whatever they serve here. Stay in here, though, okay?"

I nodded and clutched Duckie to my chest, rather shocked she was leaving me. She walked briskly into the milling crowd, leaving me alone.

There had to be over fifty people in the room, all of them dressed up and talking quietly. A few looked at me curiously, but no one came over. I think I was happy about that, though I wasn't sure. Biting my lip, I went in search of cookies. Mom hardly ever let me have them at home so I figured I might as well make the best of it.

The table was long with a white table cloth and covered in plates of everything from cookies, cakes, cheese, and crackers. There were coffee makers, and all that went with making it, at the far end.

Minding my manners I tucked Duckie under one arm and grabbed a paper plate. Filling it higher than I probably should have, I then searched for a quiet spot.

There weren't any. I settled for sitting on the floor between the table and a potted, fake tree.

I was half through the plate and wondering if there was anything other than coffee to drink when raised voices caught my attention. I'm used to yelling, and used to one of the voices being Mom's, but rarely in public. Peering around the tree I jammed a whole cookie in my mouth and tried to see what was going on. There were too many people and my vantage from the floor didn't help either.

I couldn't even make out what they were saying so many other people were talking. The noise continued for a while and then died off. The crowd started to thin by the time I finally managed to eat the last cookie.

I waited for Mom but saw no sign of her. After a while longer I got up and put my plate in the garbage pail by the table. Looking around the almost empty room, panic almost made me throw up. I couldn't see Mom anywhere.

I walked around the long room, even close to the closed casket. She wasn't sitting quietly anywhere. "Mom?" My steps quickened as I half ran to the door. "Mom!"

I crossed the hall and looked into the other room. It was almost empty, too, but I looked through it anyway. I held Duckie tightly to my chest. When I came out into the hall again there was a couple walking by. "Excuse me, where is the bathroom?" Maybe she was in there.

They gave me directions and I ran. I searched every stall. She wasn't there. I threw up in the toilet. At least Mom had braided my hair. I couldn't stop crying while I washed my face and hands. What had happened to her? Had she...forgotten me?

My tears wouldn't stop and my nose was running. I carried Duckie in a death-grip as I ran back to the front of the building. Maybe she would be there.

It was empty. Even the lady behind the desk was gone. A large clock on the wall behind the desk read 6:12. I walked around the room, tears burning my eyes. Eventually I stopped and curled up on one of the flowery couches. Mom had to come back. She'd see me here.

When I woke, it was dark out and someone was leaning over me. "Hey there, sweetie. Everything okay?"

I blinked up at the blond desk lady. The tears started again. "I can't find Mom!"

She patted my shoulder. "Deaths can be hard. I'm sure she's here somewhere." She looked down at her watch. "We close in an hour, I'm sure she'll find you before then. You let me know, okay?"

I nodded. "What time is it?"

"Almost eight. Are you hungry?"

I shook my head. "Can I go look for her again?"

"Of course." The woman stared after me as I walked back to the main hall, wiping my eyes and sniffling. The room we'd been in had people again, but no Mom. I slowly started checking each of the other rooms, too. There were a lot of them.

By the time I got to the end, my tears had dried up and I was exhausted. The last room looked empty but I went in to check anyways. It was smaller than the others and soon I found myself by another closed casket.

I couldn't help but stare at this one. It was brilliant white with gold handles and trim. The lights made it look like it was glowing. Why did they make them so pretty if they were going in the dirt? I held Duckie under my chin and tried not to start crying again.

"Don't be sad."

With a gasp I whirled around. An old woman sat in a chair behind me. She patted the seat next to her. I went and sat, trying not to sniffle. Smiling, she stroked my messy hair.

She was pretty, even being old. Her white hair was still thick and done up like a lady's. She had wrinkles but I could see a beautiful face underneath, made even more beautiful by her smile. Dressed all in black, I assumed she was here to pay her respects to whoever had died.

"What's wrong?"

I sniffled and then the tears started again. "I t-think Mom f-forgot me here."

The lady shook her head sadly. "Is that all? This is a place of mourning for those who have gone. A very sad place."

I felt bad and lowered my head. She was right. Someone she knew had *died*, and I was crying because I couldn't find my Mom. Still, I didn't know what to do and I was very mad at Mom. "She forgot me!"

The old woman laughed lightly and sat back in her chair. "Oh, to be a child again. With such little cares."

"I'm not little!"

She leaned forward and placed a finger against my forehead. "Being forgotten is not always a bad thing."

It burned where she touched me, and I jerked back. She laughed again, and this time I didn't like it. Her beautiful face didn't seem safe anymore. Her eyes were too dark, her smile no longer kind.

I jumped up and ran from the room, not bothering at all with manners.

"Savannah!"

I'd never been so relieved to hear Mom's frantic voice.

She wrapped her arms around me when I barreled into her. "I'm so sorry, sweetie." She held me back to look me over. "Are you alright?"

I nodded, but started crying again anyway.

"Let's get you home."

Mom apologized the entire way home, and even stopped at McDonalds to get me some dinner. I got spoiled all day Sunday, too. It didn't really make me feel better. I couldn't forget she'd forgotten me. I couldn't ignore the fight Mom and Dad had about it either when they thought I was asleep.

Dad tried to talk to me about it over and over again. I didn't want to talk. Sometimes important things are forgotten. A person will get so involved in one thing, they forget something else. Someone else. But parents aren't supposed to forget their children. Not great parents like mine. At least I'd thought they were great parents.

Finally one day I got tired of him bringing it up again and again. "Dad, stop it! Just forget about it!"

He did. Just like that.

Cool!

Giggling I bounced around the house. The things I could do! The trouble I could get away with!

That was how it all started. Looking back, I still remember how excited and thrilled I'd been when I first discovered my power.

I tested Dad later, asking shy questions about how Mom had forgotten me. He didn't remember a thing. Somehow, I'd made him forget.

You can get away with a lot when you can make people forget. My young mind quickly came up with dozens of tricks I could play and trouble to get into. Many of my evil plans I did over the next few weeks. My super hero power worked on everyone. Except for myself. I even did an experiment, writing something down (so I could check in case it did work) and then telling myself to forget. I still remembered.

It didn't take much for me to guess the scary old lady at the funeral home had done this to me. I didn't know why, but I didn't really care either. It was fun and it kept me out of trouble.

Or so I thought.

The problem with super powers is that just like in the movies, things go wrong. When I was ten I had no idea what I was doing. I didn't know my limits or even how the power really worked. I didn't realize how dangerous my power could be, or how important people's memories are.

Needless to say, it didn't take long for those horrible things to start to happen because of my overuse and carelessness. People started to forget *me*. First it was people I didn't really care about, but then I messed up and I lost my best friends. Very quickly, I tried to stop using it all together but that isn't as easy as it sounds. It turned out I didn't have to speak the words, I could think them instead. I finally understood my power was dangerous.

It happened slowly, one friend at a time. Sometimes I could make friends with them again, but I couldn't give back their memories. I spent more and more time crying in my room. I would skip school altogether most days.

Mom and Dad didn't like that. Not at all. The fighting started again and this time I knew it was about me. I wanted them to forget, but I was afraid.

I managed, for a while, to keep things mostly under control. For two years I did, until I slipped again. My teacher kicked me out of class thinking I shouldn't be there. I got so angry, things went downhill from there.

An angry teen with the power to make people forget is not a good combination. I did more stupid things. Things I regret terribly, things which put me on the road I'm on today.

I miss you Mom and Dad.

I miss you so very much.

Being forgotten is something many people fear. This story has been in my head for a long time. Well, not so much this beginning, but the story of Savannah as an older teen with this power. One of these days I'll make a clone and finally get her tale written.

The Punkin King

by

Sean Hayden

"Mom, I like this one!" Jack pointed down at a rather robust looking gourd. His mother walked over to where he stood. She looked down and gasped. The pumpkin prices this year were astounding. The one at her little boy's feet had to weigh at least twenty-five pounds. She quickly did the math in her head and groaned at the price. Twelve dollars for a pumpkin was just a little more than she was willing to spend.

"Jack, that one's a little too heavy, baby. Come on. Let's go find another."

"No, Mommy. I want *this* one. It perdy."

"Jack, I said no. Come on." She reached down and grabbed his pudgy little hand. She tried to pull him away from the pumpkin, but he stood rooted to the ground. She yanked again but couldn't budge him. She looked at his face as he just stared at the pumpkin smiling. "Jack?"

"Yes, Mommy?"

"Come on, sweetie. Let's go find a prettier pumpkin," Nancy said nervously.

"No, Mommy. I like this one and it really wants to go home with us." Jack bent down and picked the pumpkin up off the ground without any trouble at all. Nancy's mouth opened in shock.

"Okay, baby. We'll get this one, but let me carry it." Nancy bent down and touched her hands to the smooth surface of the pumpkin. She hissed in shock as the orange flesh burned her skin. "What the hell?"

"Are you okay, Mommy?"

Nancy looked at her hands. The flesh wasn't even pink. It showed no signs of burns either. She shook her head and chalked the feeling up to being overtired. "I'm fine, sweetie," she said and reached down to take the pumpkin again. She noticed Jack's little smile as he watched her hands. She paused midway. "Are you sure you can carry such a big pumpkin, Jack?"

"I'm sure, Mommy."

She shrugged her shoulders and led her five year old son to the check out register. It had been set up at the entrance to the tented pumpkin patch. Every year they'd stop at the same place along the old highway that led from Lazy Days Daycare center to their tiny two bedroom house on the outskirts of town.

"That's a mighty fine pumpkin you got there, son. You picked out a winner," the old man behind the register said. He reached down with gloved hands and plucked the massive gourd from the hands of Jack and set it on a large silver scale. The red needle swooped from zero to thirty five pounds.

Nancy stared at Jack in shock. "So much for twelve dollars," she muttered under her breath.

"That will be three dollars, ma'am."

Nancy stopped digging through her purse for a twenty dollar bill and stared at the man like he had grown an extra head. She opened her mouth to say something but just smiled instead. She pulled out a five and handed it to him. She looked back at the scale. The needle had settled right on the six pound mark. She rubbed her eyes to make sure she'd read it right and then at the large pumpkin on the scale. "No wonder he could carry it," she whispered and looked down at a smiling Jack.

"Here's your change, ma'am." The old man smiled and handed her two dollars. She pocketed the change and picked up the pumpkin to hand to Jack. She nearly dropped it. It weighed more than her son did.

"Careful, ma'am. They can get slippery."

She turned and nodded wide-eyed at the man. Jack reached up and took the pumpkin like it weighed no more

94

than an inflatable beach ball. She stared at him as he ran toward their green minivan.

They made the trip home in record time. Nancy shut off the radio because she couldn't find a decent song to save her life. Instead she smiled and listened to Jack as he rambled on like he was having a conversation with the pumpkin strapped into the seat next to him.

By the time they pulled into the driveway she was starting to worry. Jack's conversation had turned into a full blown, one sided argument. Apparently the pumpkin was winning, too.

"Fine. Be that way," Jack yelled and slammed the back door shut after he got out, leaving the pumpkin alone in the back seat.

"Are you going to carry your pumpkin inside, Jack?"

"No! He wants you to carry him in," he said and stormed into the house.

Nancy shrugged and took it from the seat. She strained to get it inside the house, but she finally managed. Jack sat on the couch watching cartoons about undersea creatures with annoying voices. Nancy personally hated the show. "Are you going to help me carve it?"

"Carve what?"

"The pumpkin. Tomorrow's Halloween. We won't have time to carve it after you get home from scho–" The look of horror on Jack's face stopped Nancy from finishing her sentence.

"Carve it? Carve it? Mommy you can't kill Necrostophiles," Jack said slowly, stumbling over the name.

"Necrowho?"

"Stophiles. That's his name. If you kill him the other punkins will be very mad."

"Okay, Jack. Why don't you go get into bed? You've got a big day tomorrow. School and then trick or treats."

Jack nodded and hugged his mother. She helped him get is pajamas on and got him tucked in. "G'night, Mommy."

"Goodnight, Jackie. Sweet dreams," she said and flipped the light switch by his door.

She made her way into the kitchen and poured herself a glass of red wine. She managed not to spill the over-full glass as she made her way back to the small living-room. She sighed wearily as she sat down on the couch in the spot Jack had vacated. She took a sip, realized she was watching cartoons, and flipped on the news. Story after story threatened to send her mood spiraling into the abyss. "The crazies are out early this year."

She flipped off the TV, checked on the sleeping Jack, and made her way back into the kitchen. She drained the rest of her wine and set the empty glass on the kitchenette table holding Necrowhateverhisnamewas. She gave the pumpkin the middle finger and put her hands on her hips. She stared at it for a full minute before deciding she'd had enough. She opened the drawer under the microwave and pulled out a serrated kitchen knife.

She walked over to the pumpkin and put the tip of the knife about three inches from the stem. She smiled as she drove the blade into the pumpkin all the way to the hilt. The pumpkin screamed. Maybe it was her. Either way, she let go of the handle and backed up against the kitchen counter behind her. Blood, as red as the wine that had been in her glass, began pouring freely from the wound in the top of the pumpkin.

A low moaning noise filled her ears as the blood formed a pool on the table and began falling to the floor in a miniature red waterfall. Nancy turned to run and saw

Jack standing in the entrance to the kitchen looking very angry.

"Mommy, I told you *no!*" He ran over to the pumpkin and began rubbing his hand gently over it and whispering to it softly. Nancy screamed and grabbed Jack's arm. She tried to yank him away, but just like at the pumpkin patch, she couldn't move him. He looked up at her and a single tear slid down his cheek. "You killed him, Mommy. I asked you not to, but you did it anyway. The others are coming. I won't stop them either.

"Who's coming?"

"The other punkins. You killed their king."

Nancy put her hands over her mouth and stifled a scream as the first vine shot through the kitchen window. She ducked as it shot straight for her. She managed to dodge it, but a second, thicker vine managed to wrap itself around her neck. She grasped futilely at it as it kept tightening. Fighting to breathe, she reached into the drawer next to her and grabbed a butcher knife. She slashed at the vine and cut through it with one swing. The vine slipped from her neck. She ran back to Jack to grab him and run. She stopped before she touched him. His skin had turned a dark, brownish-green. His face started turning orange. His eyes glowed like twin candles and his nose sank into his face. He opened his mouth and flames flashed between his shrinking lips as his mouth curled in an insanely large smile that spread from ear to ear. She watched as her tiny son began to grow before her eyes. He towered over her, at least seven feet tall.

She started screaming.

Jack's skeletal brown hand wrapped around her throat.

"I begged you not to kill him, Mommy," he said in a demonic voice. "Now I am the Punkin King."

Lately, I've been having some seriously sleepless nights. I blame it on all the stress on my life. While the lack of sleep isn't very beneficial to my sanity, it does help me come up with some outrageous stories. I wrote this one around Halloween. I write a lot of horror, but I've been focusing a lot more on writing steampunk. I was feeling a little nostalgic for some creepy stories, so I penned The Punkin King. I fell asleep right after with a grin on my face that spread from ear to ear. I do so love Halloween.

Excerpt from Ring Around the Rosie
by Jen Wylie

Aaron squinted up into the afternoon sun. Shielding his brown eyes with one hand he searched the sky for clouds. Only brilliant blue filled his field of vision. Apparently the June heat wave wasn't going to end today.

He puffed his dark brown hair off his face as he continued his slow walk home, swinging his flute case gently as he tramped along the quiet streets. He stopped when he reached the large community park, scanning the playground and surrounding area to see if his mother and little sister were still there. They had walked with him as far as the park on his way to his music lesson, but his mother had warned him they might return home if his sister got cranky from the heat.

He didn't see them on the large play structures or running about the areas of open grass. He continued along the sidewalk, pausing as he neared the small wooded area of the park. A few people sat under the large maples and oaks at its edge. He couldn't see further into the trees, shadows and low growth blocked his view. However, he could hear the laughter and screams of kids as they played within the cool shade.

Wiping the sweat from his forehead he started off again, only to stop once more at the faint sound of music coming from the woods. The melody was sweet yet haunting. He didn't recognize the song, or even the instrument playing it. *Some sort of pipes.* He couldn't think of any of the local radio stations that would play that type of song. The music stopped a moment before continuing again. His eyebrows went up in surprise. *Someone was actually playing it?* He debated going to check it out and glanced down at his watch. It was getting close to dinner and if he arrived home late his mother would freak out.

With a grimace he started home again, the beautiful, haunting tune repeating itself in his head. He began to hum it softly as he walked with a small smile on his lips. It was simple, yet catchy. He liked it.

Excerpt from The Games We Play
by Sean Hayden

"Are you okay?" He leaned forward and put his hand over hers. She tried not to pull away. She gasped at the coldness of his touch. His skin felt different, too. Even the toughest of construction workers have meaty parts to their hand. Soft and pliable flesh. His hand felt more like stone than skin. She couldn't help herself, her other hand made its way on top of his and she slid her fingers over the back of his hand. It was perfectly smooth. She could feel the bumps of the veins under his skin, but no pores, no hair, or even wrinkles marred their perfect surface. She gasped and looked up at him.

He glared down at her and she watched the evil smile make its way back onto his perfect lips. "Are you afraid?" His voice was just above a whisper yet she heard him perfectly, even over the din of the crowded bar.

She quickly tried to pull her hands away, but she only succeeded in saving one of them. The one still in his hand was trapped in his grip of stone. She looked around frantically, thinking of calling for help, but his grip tightened. She let out a little mew and it stopped. She looked at Charles, her captor, and he chuckled again. This time she didn't need to fight off the effects of his laugh, her fear did it for her.

"Yes," she managed to answer his question.
"Yes, what?"

"Yes, I'm afraid. What are you?"

"You know the answer to that one, my fair Veronica," he said and for the first time she saw the dim bar room lights glisten off his fangs.

"V–v–vam…"

"Pire," he finished and smiled as she sucked in a big gulp of air.

Other Works by Jen Wylie

Ring Around the Rosie (short story)

Jump (short story)

Sweet Light (novel)
Dark Madness (novel-coming soon!)

Broken Aro (novel-coming Oct 2012)

Immortal Echoes
-The Forgotten Echo (novella)
-The Untouchable Echo (novella)

Tales of Ever (YA novella series)
-Banished
-Fire Girl
-Shadow Boy
-The Lost Tree
-Dragon Rising
-Sanctuary

Jen Wylie's Biography

Jennifer Wylie resides in rural Ontario, Canada with her two boys, Australian shepherd, a flock of birds and a disagreeable amount of wildlife. In a cosmic twist of fate she dislikes the snow and cold.

Before settling down to raise a family, she attained a BA from Queens University and worked in retail and sales. Thanks to her mother she acquired a love of books at an early age and began writing in public school. She constantly has stories floating around in her head, and finds it amazing most people don't. Jennifer writes various forms of fantasy, both novels and short stories. Sweet light is her debut novel.

www.jenniferwylie.ca

Other works by Sean Hayden

The Demonkin Series:
-Origins
-Deceptions

My Soul to Keep (Coming Soon)

The Magnificent Steam Carnival of Professor Pelusian
Minus Series: (Co-authored with Connor Hayden)
-First Flight
-Second Chance
-Third Time\
-Fourth Stand (Coming Soon)

Lady Dorn

The Games We Play

Her Majesty's Mysterious Conveyance (Anthology)
-Queen of the Travelers

A Very Scary Christmas (Anthology)
-The Ghost of Christmas Last

Sean Hayden's Biography

Born the son of a fire chief, Sean naturally developed a love of playing with fire. His family and friends quickly found other outlets for his destructive creativity. Writing is his latest endeavor.

Always a fan of the macabre, mythical, and magical, Sean found a love of urban fantasy and horror. After writing several novels in this genre, he found, fell in love with, and immersed himself in steampunk. He has always wanted to rewrite history and steampunk gave him that opportunity.

Sean currently lives in Florida as a fiber-optic engineer as well as an author. He was blessed with the two most amazing children he could ever hope for, has met the absolute love of his life, who coincidentally is his partner in everything. His hobbies include grand designs on world domination as well as a starring role in his own television sitcom.

www.seanhayden.org